THE
MUMWALDS

THE MUMWALDS

Lee A. Crawford

Chalice Press
St. Louis, Missouri

Illustrations: Doug Hall

Art Director: Michael Dominguez

10 9 8 7 6 5 4 3 2 1

Library of Congress Cataloging–in–Publication Data

Crawford, Lee A.
    The Mumwalds / by Lee A. Crawford.
     ISBN 0-8272-2322-6
     I. Title.
    PS3553.R285M86 1994   813'.54   93-23432

Printed in the United States of America

To my wife
Margaret
for her support
and to
Beethoven
for his inspiration.

Contents

1 Introduction   1

2 The Problem   5

3 An Abortive Solution   12

4 The Ceremony of the Star   22

5 Troubling Questions   26

6 Questions Persist   37

7 A Startling Revelation   42

8 An Irritated Sage   49

9 A Startling Discovery   57

10 Captain's Report   64

11 The Way of the Chipmunk   72

12 An Unfriendly Reception   77

13 Escape   85

14 Rescue   93

15 New Revelations from the Past   105

16 The Trial   113

17 Dumbell and Dissension   125

18 Revenge Mission   131

19 Mission for Salvation   139

20 The Ceremony of War   143

21 Ambush   152

22 The End of Sage   159

23 Suicide?   168

24 Toward the Unknown   175

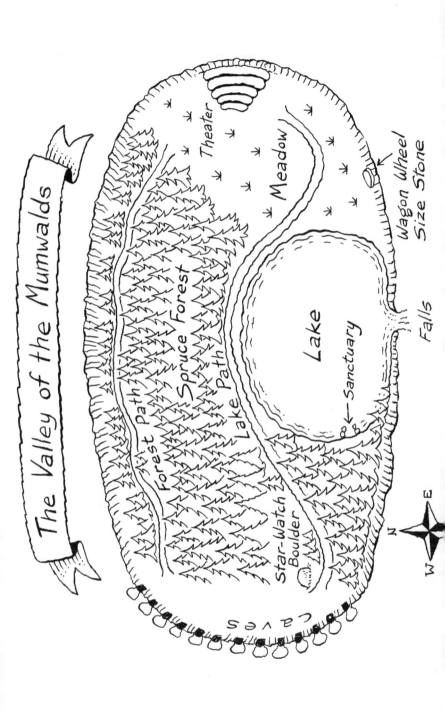

The Valley of the Mumwalds

Theater

Meadow

Wagon Wheel Size Stone

Forest Path

Spruce Forest

Lake Path

Lake

Sanctuary

Falls

Star-Watch Boulder

Caves

N E W S

1

Introduction

Along the unpredictable road of evolutionary process there have been many pauses. For a few, too-brief moments in the cosmic expanse of time, some pauses have shown wonderful promise. Idyllic conditions have flourished for a few centuries and intelligent life, flowering under these conditions, has responded by helping to shape ways of life only dreamed about in our world today. Unfortunately, travel on the road inevitably continues, often with disastrous effects on these ways of life.

Ages ago, before human beings had developed to the point they have reached in the last few thousand years, intelligence and awareness very much like that of humans arose in a naturally isolated valley of a heavily forested, mountainous region of what are now called the Rocky Mountains of North America. The creatures who exhibited these humanlike traits were a curious-looking lot. They called themselves Mumwalds.

Adult Mumwalds looked much like small, rounded boulders, spheres perhaps a foot in diameter. No heads perched on top of the spheres. What would have to be called the front of each ball had the features of a human face, more or less. The lips were as red as a cardinal's feathers, the nose was a little pink pebble, and the two eyes were bright blue in the males and green in the females. The males were covered with a very fine, very white fur. The fur of the females was a medium gray.

Two arms protruded awkwardly from the sides of each sphere, one on either side of the face. They were usually just long enough for the pudgy fingers of one hand to grab hold of the fingers of the other in front of the mouth. Mumwalds' stubby legs were only about six inches long and ended in large, ducklike webbed feet. No ears were visible, but each sphere had hearing mechanisms that could be called ears, located underneath the fur and skin above where each arm protruded.

The technological advancement of Mumwald culture was extremely primitive. In many respects, they lived as we normally picture life of the caveman, with two significant differences. First, because their egg-shaped valley had vertical cliffs hundreds of feet high virtually all the way around, the only predator from the animal kingdom that had access to the rotund morsels were the eagles that nested near the cliff top and occasionally swooped down to menace a young Mumwald. The only other physical threats to Mumwalds were such natural dangers as falling rocks, lightning, freezing temperatures, disease, and, of course, old age. Second, interpersonal (and it *is* appropriate to call them persons) relationships had been honed to the point that harmony reigned supreme among Mumwalds year in and year out. Oh, petty differences still erupted into minor squabbles every now and then, but no serious crimes had been committed by any Mumwald against another, or against any other creature for that matter, for generations. Furthermore, Mumwalds felt at one with their creator and sustainer, the all-powerful Great Maker. To put the matter theologically, sin had virtually been eliminated from Mumwald society. In fact, the word *sin* had been deliberately dropped from their vocabulary generations before this story begins.

Luck in genetic development surely played a role in this remarkable achievement of virtual sinlessness. But Mumwalds had also shown a genius for molding the structure of their little society to fit their situation and their dispositions. First of all, they had developed population control to an exact discipline so that the total number of live Mumwalds at any one time never varied from two dozen by more than two or three. Secondly, one male was always given the name Sage, and he was the acknowledged leader, the primary decision maker when tough decisions had to be made. He would listen to advice from others, but after making his decision, he expected, and got, no serious quibbling or grumbling. Sage always appointed one of the other males to be Captain, who served as a kind of executive secretary, seeing that Sage's orders were carried out.

Normally, only one or two adult females were past childbearing age. If such an elder female were still healthy and active, she had the title Healer and functioned as both doctor and nurse. She knew her business, too, for she had been carefully groomed by the previous Healer, and though Mumwalds weren't advanced in sophisticated technology, they had tremendous practical wisdom. Healers could successfully treat almost any hurt or ailment a Mumwald had. When a female got too old to function as Healer, she was dubbed Ancientone and was cared for lovingly until her death.

Mumwalds all lived in small caves at the base of the cliff at the western end of the valley. They didn't live together as full families. The females of child-producing age—who were, in their adulthood, simply named Motherone, Mothertwo, and so on—each had a cave, sharing it with her progeny if she had any. Ancientone always lived with Healer. Sage and Captain had caves by themselves. The other adult males lived in pairs or, when there was an odd number, in a trio. When the time came for the population to be replenished, Sage designated which male would mate with which female, taking into consideration character traits and how particular males and females felt about each other. The young were considered adult when they became five years old, and Mumwalds usually died somewhere around their fifteenth year, except, of course, in rare cases of catastrophic accident or illness.

So much for a brief introduction to the Mumwalds. This is not an "anthropological" study; it is, rather, the story of the Mumwalds' baptism into tragedy, despite their virtual sinlessness, and their reaction to such tragedy.

At the point when our story begins, Mumwalds were at the peak of the most blissful period in their history. No Mumwald had met an untimely death for ten generations. Falling boulders had missed them, violent storms and subfreezing temperatures had found them secure in their caves with plenty of provisions to wait out the bad weather, and food had been abundant year-round. Even the eagles, whose shadows sometimes passed ominously over them, had been frustrated. Adult Mumwalds were too heavy for these eagles to carry away, and young Mumwalds were never allowed to wander far from an adult. Natural death was an accepted fact of life, bringing with it sorrow in those still living, but not causing deep-rooted anxiety. Life was simple and fulfilling, and when it had been allowed to run its proper course, death was no threat.

2

The Problem

One early morning in a mid-summer during this period, Sage sat musing in the cool, calm air at the mouth of his cave, his mind relaxed and clear. The sky was cloudless. It would be some time before the sun rose high enough for its rays to brighten the tops of the tall spruce trees in front of the caves.

Sage loved this valley. It had everything the Mumwalds could possibly want. Though he didn't know it, the valley was an odd geological phenomenon. With its oval shape and high cliff sides, it looked much like a volcanic crater, but it wasn't. The rock was granite, not lava, and plant and small animal life flourished on the valley floor. The floor was about a half mile long and a quarter mile wide. Only one break spoiled the otherwise continuous cliff that rose around it. The break was a deep, narrow cut in the southern wall. The cut ran clear to the valley floor and served as a spillway for the beautiful, spring-fed mountain lake, about two hundred yards in diameter, that lay against the southern wall. This spillway was not a route by which Mumwalds could leave the valley, nor could invaders use it to enter, for the light stream of water that flowed out of the lake dropped immediately another two hundred feet, forming a misty, thin waterfall that no Mumwald in memory had ever seen. They only knew that the water fell and that they dared not get too close to the cut or the current would pull them over.

Most of the rest of the valley was covered by a thick, healthy spruce forest. From his cave mouth, Sage looked out on the smaller of the two clearings in the valley. This clearing was a rough, cracked rock ledge, kept clear of plants and of loose rocks that sloughed off the cliff above. The other clearing, at the eastern end of the valley, was much larger, nearly the size of the lake but not as round. Many kinds of plants grew in that meadow, and these various species were carefully nurtured, for many of them provided the substances that Healer used in her treatments of illnesses and injuries.

Sage absentmindedly reached into a small pile of pine cones he had brought out with him. Without looking at what he was doing, he let his fingers find the softest cone. This is the way he liked them, picked young when they were tender and pliable. Most adults got to the point where they preferred cones that were harder, even ones that had already released their seeds. As far as Mumwalds' gastrointestinal systems were concerned, the stage of a cone's development didn't matter. Strong mouth and stomach juices quickly worked all cones into a digestible, nutritious glob. But Sage liked each bite with his strong teeth to mash deep into the cone and tear off a big chunk of soft cone flesh. He hated the sound and the feel of hard cones crackling and crunching in his mouth.

He was reflecting on the good fortune that Mumwalds and their animal companions, the chipmunks and mice and birds and trout, experienced in their protected valley home. No trace of pride or gloating tainted his feelings, only satisfaction and gratitude that everything was going well. Lurking in the recesses of his mind were tales—perhaps legendary, perhaps

perhaps not—of times when Mumwalds had known a much wider world and had been rudely buffeted by harsh conditions, but he kept these memories pushed to the edge of awareness. Only sages knew these tales, and Sage was not even sure why the stories were passed on from one sage to the next. It didn't matter. He didn't plan to darken the days of his contemporaries by telling them any of the stories. Whenever a young Mumwald expressed curiosity about what might be beyond this valley, Sage brushed off the query with some such answer as, "It doesn't matter so long as we are left to ourselves to prosper as we are." Most Mumwalds happily pranced away, in so far as they *could* prance, upon hearing such an answer.

The light flapping of webbed feet on stone alerted Sage that someone else was awake. He twisted his sphere to the left and watched as another adult male paddled up to him, rubbing his eyes with his fat fingers to get the sleep out of them. "Good morning, Dumbell," said Sage quietly.

"Yup. Yup," said Dumbell. He yawned and stretched, bringing his fists back down to drum several beats near the top of his sphere. "Out with night, in with bright. Got to work, mustn't shirk," he muttered. Then he yawned again and stood still beside Sage.

"What is your task this morning, Dumbell?" asked Sage in a gentle tone.

"Yup, I'm the path cleaner all right. That's what I am. Yup."

"Is the lake path here the one Captain wanted you to start on?"

"Yup, my good man, that's the one."

"Well?"

Dumbell stared at the benign smile on the old Mumwald's face for a few seconds before mumbling, "Okey, dokey." He stepped off the low ledge that lay in front of the caves and began to pick up sticks and stones that had fallen or been kicked into the dirt and needle pathway. It took him only moments to get into the swing of the job. As he merrily tossed unwanted objects to his right and left, he began quietly singing his work song. The words brought an even bigger smile to Sage's face.

A trout and a flea and three blind mice
Were sittin' on a pine cone countin' lice.
The trout slipped, fell on the flea;
"Oops," said the flea, "there's a trout on me!"

Boom, boom, ain't it great to be crazy,
Boom, boom, ain't it great to be crazy,
Silly and foolish all day long,
Boom, boom, ain't it great to be crazy.

A couple of hours later Dumbell was singing and working his jolly way along the path directly by the lake. Mothertwo and Motherfour came strolling up behind him with their three young ones, followed closely by two adult males, Jester and Muscles. Dumbell paid no attention to the fact that a crowd was coming. He gaily kept throwing sticks and stones every which way. He was no longer careful to see that they landed off the path. One small stick flew high into the air and came

down right on the top of the sphere of young Mischief, Mothertwo's lemon-sized baby, who could walk and talk, as could all Mumwalds at this age, even though he was only a few months old.

"Owww!" howled the little fellow. Without giving his mother time to find out what had happened, Mischief hopped to the edge of the lake. He scooped up a tiny wad of juicy mud and let it fly at Dumbell. The path cleaner was just turning around to see what all the yelling was about. The mud ball smacked him square in the nose. He was so startled he couldn't say a thing. Then he got a glint in his eye and a happy smile on his face and headed for the mud himself. There was no question about what he had in mind.

"Dumbell! Don't you dare!" shouted Mothertwo. Her shout met unhearing ears. Dumbell formed a huge mud ball, almost as big as Mischief himself, and let it fly. His aim was as weak as his mind. Instead of hitting his little attacker, his missile slopped into the side of Mothertwo.

That fine lady stood rigid, with her chubby fists clenched. "Dumbell! Look what you've done!"

Mischief dodged behind his mother. Muscles, Jester, Motherfour, and the other two youngsters waited tensely, but hopefully, for the scene to unfold.

Mothertwo's momentary anger didn't phase Dumbell. He reached down, gathered up more mud, and offered it to her. "Come, my fair lady. Won't you join us in a bit of sport?"

Mothertwo's face relaxed. A gleam came into her eye, too. With a slight, gracious bow, she accepted the mud from Dumbell and immediately sloshed it right back in his face. That was the signal all the others had been hoping for. Everyone jumped for the mud. They began scooping up batches as fast as they could and slinging them in every direction. No one took sides. For a good fifteen minutes everyone flung mud at whoever was closest. One of Muscles' larger globs completely covered Mischief, but the feisty little fighter simply shook himself and re-entered the fray with renewed fury. Everyone was laughing in the Mumwalds' peculiar, deep, croaking laugh, sounding like a bunch of frogs gone berserk. When everyone was tired and thoroughly coated with mud, Dumbell went over to Mothertwo and offered her his hand, like a gallant knight. "Shall we bathe together in the lake, my fair lady?" Then they all swam out into the lake and splashed water on each other. In many ways, they looked more at home in the water than on land. Their webbed feet made their movements smooth and adroit in the water, in sharp contrast to their awkward waddle on land.

As they were getting the last bits of mud out of their coats, Sage and Captain appeared on the path from the caves. They moved very slowly, for the black-streaked old leader's joints were stiff and sore. Sage spoke as they approached. "Ah, I told you, Captain, all that ruckus we heard was from a jolly mud fight. But we've missed the fun."

The two high officials came up to the site of the fight and surveyed the mud-spattered boulders, path, and trees. Sage reached out to a low lying spruce branch and plucked off a mud-covered cone. "Here, Captain, wash this off," he said. "We mustn't spoil food."

Captain went to the edge of the lake and swished the cone in the water. He stepped back up on the path and handed the cone toward Sage.

"No, no," said Sage. "That's not the kind I like. We'll just take it back to storage. Wait! Hold that out here again. Let me have a look." Captain handed him the cone. Sage examined it carefully, slowly turning it over and around several times.

"What is it?" asked Captain. The others, out of the water now, helped him form a semicircle facing Sage.

"I'm not sure," said Sage. "Some parts of this cone seem to have a strange orange cast. I've never seen anything quite like it. And those parts feel slightly more fuzzy than the rest."

"Uh huh, I see," said Captain. "Here, let me taste one of those parts." He took the cone and crunched into it with his mouth. Before even taking a chew, he spit it out, his tongue sputtering and working frantically to get the last little bits out. "The taste is terrible, Sage."

"Hmmm. Yes, that was obvious."

"Yup. I could tell you didn't like it," said Dumbell with a knowing smile.

Sage immediately asked his fellow Mumwalds if they had found any other cones like this one but just hadn't mentioned it. Dumbell stared at the ground but said nothing. No one did. Sage then led them along the path. They stopped at each low spruce branch they came to and examined the cones on it. The strange orange blight had infected at least one cone on most branches. On some branches several cones were blotched with it. Memories stirred in Sage's mind, memories of one of the tales of old that the previous sage had told him. It spoke of the sudden onset of a spruce cone disease and of the famine and suffering that resulted. He needed time to dredge that memory fully. He dismissed all but Captain and asked him to escort him back to his cave.

After an hour of quiet reflection, Sage was ready to share his thoughts on the problem with everyone. He called to Captain and asked him to inform all the Mumwalds that a gathering would be held at straight-up sun time at the theater.

3

An Abortive Solution

The theater was actually a series of four rock ledges at the base of the cliff at the eastern end of the valley. Long ago, Mumwalds had cleaned off and smoothed down the surfaces to use as seats in a natural amphitheater. At the designated time, all the Mumwalds were seated except for Jester and another adult male, Sneaky. Sage looked up at the sun impatiently and then turned to look down the lake path to see if the two late ones were coming.

Suddenly, Jester came stumbling out of the path that led through the thick forest on the northern side of the valley. "Help me! Help me!" he cried. "Sneaky fell over on the path. He can't get up!"

Sage whirled around, all irritation gone from his face. "Calmly, my son, calmly. Healer, go with him and attend to Sneaky."

Healer had already risen. She picked up her basket woven from reeds and was on her way. Jester led her to the spot where Sneaky lay on his back, his glazed blue eyes staring blankly at the tree branches. His lips were a pale pink. Stubby limbs dangled limply from his round body.

Healer looked him over carefully and stroked his soft, white fur. "Were you two eating freshly picked cones?"

Since Sneaky gave no indication of hearing the question, Jester answered, "Natch, we're always eating. Nothing wrong with a good, fresh cone when you feel like it, is there?"

"Maybe there is," said Healer, giving Jester a puzzled look. "Didn't you know what the gathering we are supposed to be having right now is about?"

"Heck, no. We got the word about being there from Dumbell, but he didn't say why. We just figured we were in for a little entertainment—though I was curious why I hadn't been asked to tell a few jokes."

"Your jokes are…but, no, we must see to Sneaky." Healer rummaged through her basket. She pulled out a thistle leaf and held it up. "Tradition instructed me always to keep a reasonably fresh one of these in my basket, but I've never had to use one." She tore off a tiny section of the leaf and forced it into Sneaky's mouth. Within seconds Sneaky's whole body jerked in a violent spasm. He rolled over nearly onto his face and struggled to lift his sphere off the ground, using both arms and both legs. Finally, he got into position on all fours with his face looking straight into the loose dirt he had been lying in. Another convulsion wrenched his body. A gurgling sound erupted from deep inside his sphere and out of his mouth spurted the remains of the cones he had recently eaten. He slowly edged sideways on all fours so that he didn't have to continue staring at the mess he had made. Healer was close beside him, gently rubbing his side.

"Was there an odd taste to any of the cones when you ate them?" she asked.

Sneaky rocked his sphere forward and backward in a nod but still said nothing.

"Why didn't you spit it out immediately?" Healer said in a mildly scolding tone.

Sneaky's body shook slightly. When he didn't answer, Jester again did. "We were having a contest to see who could eat the most cones before a bluebird flew off a branch. Sneaky doesn't like to lose, so he probably just gulped the bad tasting cone down and went on to the next. What difference does it make how the cones taste, anyway?"

"I'm not sure," said Healer. "That's what the gathering is about. Here, help me get Sneaky up on his legs. We'll cut through the forest straight to the lake. He should be all right once he gets some fresh water to complete the treatment."

* * *

The Mumwalds back at the theater were sitting in silence. The urgency and anxiety in Jester's voice and demeanor had stunned them. Sage didn't want to say anything until everyone was present. He, too, sat quietly, waiting for some word from the three missing Mumwalds.

One Mumwald, tiny Mischief, did not let the shock hold him in inaction for too long, however. While his mother gazed meditatively into the trees, he surreptitiously picked up a little rock. He positioned it on his thumb, with his forefinger holding it in place. With a quick flick of the finger, the rock shot straight at Punky, Mothersix's two-year-old male.

"Eeee!" squealed Punky.

Mothertwo twisted to look down at her son. Mischief's lips were pressed closed and his eyes squinted in a suppressed smile. The good mother instantly snatched the devilish little fellow up by his tiny feet and held him upside down.

Sage glared up at them from his seat on the lowest level. "Mothertwo, do you have the situation under control?"

"Yes, Sage. I'm sorry for the disturbance."

"Humph. I don't like serious assemblies bothered by rascally play."

The embarrassed Mothertwo continued to hold Mischief upside down until the top of his body—which was now on the bottom, of course—grew a bright pink that could be seen right through his white fur. It was quite a painful condition for a Mumwald and usually more than enough punishment to make little Mumwalds behave.

Mothersix leaned over to ask the cannonball-sized Punky what had happened. After she had heard him out, she spoke to him earnestly for a few seconds, then spoke quietly to Sage, "We recognize that our response was not appropriate, Sage. After the gathering is finished, Punky will be confined to our cave until the shadow of the cliff reaches halfway up the tallest tree in front of our cave."

Sage nodded his thanks and returned to his private thoughts. Within a few minutes Sneaky and Jester walked into view on the lake path, with Healer close behind. The assembled Mumwalds watched the three as they approached through the meadow, their tops only sticking inches above the sea of pale blue flax swaying slightly in the breeze. All seemed normal. The theater suddenly came alive with whispers of Mumwalds expressing their relief to their neighbors.

When they came to the theater, Sneaky and Jester immediately found spaces on ledges. Healer waddled over to Sage and spoke privately with him for a few minutes before she, too, found a seat. Sage faced the audience with a grave expression, making him look even older than he was. His memory hadn't revealed much useful information. He quickly summarized what few facts were known about the orange curse on the cones. When he finished, he asked for input from anyone who might have a question, comment, or observation that had escaped the others. No one spoke up.

Finally, Captain said, "Probably no one's noticed because most of us have been eating from the stockpiles in the caves. No one has been assigned to cone-gathering duty for several weeks because we had an oversupply in the caves. It's too bad that...uh, Dumbell, did you have something to say?"

"Yup." He didn't go on.

"Well, what is it?"

"I seen one of them orange cones 'bout a week ago. Yup, I did. And I've seen a lot more since then. Yup, I have."

Hissing whispers rose from the rest of the audience. Perplexed glares focused on the confessor. Sage held up a hand, waiting to speak only after everyone had quieted down. "Why didn't you report this sooner?"

"I thought they was pretty."

"So? Why didn't you show these pretty things to some-one?"

"I was going to. Yup, I was. But I wanted to get a whole bunch first. I've been hiding all the ones I found near the path. Behind a tree. Near the lake. It's a real pretty batch, all orangish brown. I was going to give them to…to…someone." A sheepish grin came over his face. He lowered his eyes and bowed his sphere to stare at the ground.

Mischief, precocious in his understanding of relation-ships, squealed, "Dumbell has a girlfriend. Dumbell has a—" Mothertwo's hand clamped over the front of the tiny sphere.

Sage shook his head resignedly and spoke soothingly. "Thank you for that information, Dumbell. We can be fairly sure from what you say that the blight has not been here long. Perhaps it is only on the lower branches. If so, we can pick off the infected cones, take them out into the lake, and send them over the waterfall. We must make a close inspection of the upper parts of several trees."

All eyes turned immediately toward Motherone. The young mother's left arm nestled a small bundle of gray fur close to her side. "I'm afraid Climber's fast asleep, Sage," she whis-pered. "Should I wake her?"

"Not yet." With an amused tone, he addressed the audi-ence. "Practically every day we hear Motherone scolding her little daughter for doing exactly what she was named for. She is the only one of us Mumwalds who has the skill and lacks the fear to climb our trees. And she is yet small enough to go far out on the limbs where the cones grow. We shall turn Climber's bad habit into a benefit for all of us." He spoke then directly to Motherone. "Would that be acceptable to you?"

"I would be honored, Sage."

Sage immediately dismissed the assembly. Motherone gently woke Climber. The other furry creatures began milling around, conversing excitedly but in low tones. Sage waited for Motherone to bring her tiny daughter down to him, then explained to her what they wanted her to do.

Climber looked guiltily up at her mother. "But I don't want another scolding in front of all the others," she said, whimpering.

Motherone picked up the little fur ball and hugged her. "Now, now, Climber. You don't understand. Climbing is no longer wrong. It is right. You will be praised for doing it if you can throw down lots of cones from high in the trees."

"And you won't hold me upside down for being bad?"

"Of course not."

Climber was finally convinced that her favorite pastime would not get her into trouble. She slipped out of her mother's arms to the ground, hopped once straight up in the air, and took off in a floppy run toward the nearest tree with low branches. The older Mumwalds ambled along behind her, easily keeping up with her running. At the edge of the meadow, where the forest path entered the trees, Climber stopped abruptly at a tree trunk, touching the trunk without saying a word. She looked questioningly back and up at the large spheres hovering over her. Captain nodded, took a step forward, and boosted Climber onto the lowest branch. The Mumwalds watched in awe as the little ball deftly pulled herself up through the closely packed limbs until she was several feet off the ground. She started to move out toward the end of a branch, leaning forward so that her hands could grasp the branch as she worked her way out.

"No, no, my dear," said Sage. "You must go much higher. We want to inspect cones from near the tops of the trees."

Climber fearlessly backed up until her bottom bumped against the trunk. She climbed swiftly until she was only a few feet from the top of the tree. The Mumwalds on the ground could no longer see her by looking up through the multitude of branches. They moved out from under the tree and into the meadow to observe her movements. The limbs at her height were quite slender. As she moved outward on one, it bent precariously.

"Careful, little one."

"Don't worry," she called. "They bend but they don't break. And I hold on tight." Her webbed feet were abnormally flexible, for they nearly wrapped around the branch, giving her a much firmer grip than appeared possible. She was not a lot bigger than the cone she reached for at the tip of the branch. With a

twist of one small hand, she plucked the first cone and lobbed it down toward her mother. Motherone raised both arms straight up in a feeble attempt to catch it. It hit her harmlessly above the eyes and bounced over to the feet of Sage. The old leader's face tensed as he leaned over to pick it up.

"Ah," he said, as he turned it over and over. "Ah, this one is free of the malicious orange." He looked upward toward the gray spot and spoke happily, "Excellent, little one, excellent. Now move from branch to branch and throw down more until we tell you to stop."

Climber was having the time of her young life. The exhilaration of being up so high and being free from the threat of reprimand was almost too much. When a new limb was not far below the one she was on, she swung down to it, rather than backing to the trunk and cautiously climbing down. As each cone fell, a Mumwald picked it up and took it to Sage for inspection. The first six cones were free of the blight.

Climber moved out to the tip of another branch, reaching for an especially large cone. Everyone's eyes were fixed on her. Just as she twisted loose the cone and let it fall, a shadow passed swiftly over the crowd on the ground. All spheres tilted back a notch. Fear froze their stares. Their mouths lay half open, unable to utter a sound.

There it was! The dreaded bald eagle, its wings spread wide, swooping down from its nest in the craggy heights, its talons still held up against its body, its ferocious beak pointing directly at Climber.

Captain shook off his shock. "Climber! Look out! Above you!"

The little female twisted her body as far as she could and looked upward out of the corner of her eye. The eagle began braking with its wings and extended its deadly talons downward.

"Rocks! Sticks! Anything you can throw!" shouted Captain. Mumwalds scattered, frantically searching for missiles. Several rocks and stones were lofted into the air, but they didn't even reach as high as Climber. Mumwalds' short, stubby arms were not made for power throwing.

Climber kept her hands and feet grasping the limb and swiveled down underneath it, hanging from all fours like a monkey. Still the eagle descended.

"Throw harder!" shrieked Motherone.

One or two stones plopped softly against the eagle as it reached the level of the tree top. Climber squeezed her eyes closed and grasped the limb more tightly.

"Climber!" boomed Sage. "Let go! Let yourself fall!"

The great, flapping wings roared above Climber. The rush of wind swayed the branch wildly. She opened her eyes and looked into the vicious talon trap about to close on her. "Eeeee!" she screeched, and she flung wide her arms and legs.

The talons dug into the empty branch. Climber bounded off to the side of the branch below and began bouncing and sliding down through the thick spruce foliage. All the Mumwalds rushed under the tree and bunched together. Climber ricocheted off the lowest branch and fell on a bed of soft fur. Motherone scooped her daughter into her arms, and held her in a tight embrace, sobbing. Climber let out a slight whimper and snuggled close to her mother. The crowd stayed bunched tightly, sharing their warmth and life in silent gratitude.

Captain was the first to break away and go out from under the tree. The eagle was already lifting itself back up to the heights. Sage joined him, his face contorted by anguished guilt. "In our haste we were very careless, Captain. We almost lost one of our loved ones because of my foolishness. I must...."

Captain put up a hand to stop the distraught leader. Adult Mumwalds weren't shaped right to embrace each other, but Captain edged over and gave Sage reassuring rubs on the back of the old one's sphere. As they turned their attention back to the huddled Mumwalds, they got a new shock. Ancientone was lying motionless on her side, away from the others. Everyone else was watching Healer inspect Climber's bruises and scratches. The two leaders hurried over to Ancientone. Sage seized her one available arm and tugged lightly on the limp limb. Ancientone did not stir or make any sound. Captain put the inside of his wrist against her top, where a Mumwald's pulse is most prominent. He felt not even a slight beat. He shook his sphere back and forth to signal Sage.

Just then Dumbell turned around. "My good man, what's wrong with the old girl?" With that, everyone spun around and quickly encircled the fallen elder. Healer pushed her way through the crowd. After she had bent over Ancientone for a few seconds, she rose up and pronounced, "She's dead. Probably from too much excitement."

"Yup, she sure looks dead. Well, I say good-bye to a swell old gal. Yup, I do."

"Thank you, Dumbell," said Sage softly. He stared down at the gray, lifeless fur ball. Tears filled his eyes. He spoke with a quivering voice. "We averted a catastrophe only to have this sadness come upon us." He paused to collect himself and gather his thoughts. Finally, he hoarsely whispered, "Captain, take three others and carry Ancientone's body to the lakeshore. Then prepare for a Ceremony of the Star."

Captain nodded. Sage started plodding down the forest path, heading back toward his cave. Stargazer, one of the males that Captain had not asked to help, shuffled up beside him. "Sage," the younger Mumwald said, "I know this isn't a good time to show you this, but I picked up that last cone that Climber dropped just as the eagle approached."

Sage looked first into Stargazer's eyes and saw the pain and discomfort there. He reached out and patted Stargazer on the cheek. "You're the wise one. I'm glad I've chosen you to begin instruction as the next sage." The light was quite dim under the trees. Sage led his companion over to a spot where a shaft of light had found its way down to the path. He took the cone, held it in the light, and immediately saw the large orange blotch on it. Handing it back to Stargazer, he sighed deeply. "Please report this to Captain and have him send this one over the falls. We will deal with the matter tomorrow."

4

The Ceremony of the Star

After dark that evening Sage stepped to the entrance of his cave. Thousands of stars were twinkling in the clear, moonless sky. He stood silently looking up, almost as if he were in a trance.

Finally, a noise came from deep within him. At first it sounded as if he were testing his voice, trying to find just the right note. He settled on a soft but clear, low sound. "Oooooo. Oooooo. Ooo...." Still repeating it over and over, he left his cave and began walking past the other caves toward the forest path. As he passed each cave, the Mumwalds in it came out and followed behind him in single file. Each one, even the littlest, began the same moaning sound. The line slowly made its way along the dark woods path toward the theater. The valley was completely quiet except for the eerie moaning of all twenty-three remaining Mumwalds.

When the procession came out of the forest, Sage led them to the theater. He stopped on the bottom shelf, and others spread out above him. After everyone had settled, Sage ended a moan by adding a brief "aw" note. The others abruptly stopped moaning. For several minutes they all stood in silence. They were focusing their thoughts on death and the passage to the Land Beyond. When the time was right, Sage lay down on his back so that he could look straight up at the sparkling sky. The other Mumwalds followed his lead.

After several more minutes of silence, Captain began chanting quietly:

Stars, stars, so high in the sky,
Stars, stars, so bright in the night.
Stars, stars, so high in the sky,
Stars, stars, so bright in the night.

All the Mumwalds except Sage took up the chant and repeated it over and over very softly. Sage waited until the spell of the chant had time to get hold of them all. Then he spoke in a deep, steady voice that could be heard above the chanting:

O Wondrous Star,
Thou who art our carrier
To the Land Beyond,
Another of our souls
Awaits thee.

Come now, come now,
O Wondrous Star,
Keep us not waiting long.

Gather up this soul
Before the North Wind,
So cold, so brutal,
Whisks it away to No Place.
Ten nights thou hast,
For no longer can a soul
Hold against the cold tempest.

Come now, come now,
O Wondrous Star,
Keep us not waiting long.

We will watch for thee,
And when we see
That thy work is done,
Great joy will we lift to thee.

So come now, come now
O Wondrous Star,
Keep us not waiting long.

After Sage finished, the chanting slowly died away as one after the other quit. Captain was the last to stop. More silence followed. The Mumwalds anxiously watched the sky.

Suddenly, a soft thump followed by an "Ouch!" came from one of the upper shelves.

Mothertwo's voice hissed, "Mischief, get back up here."

"Don't blame me this time," whined a squeaky voice. "I was almost asleep, and I just rolled off the shelf."

Silence again. More minutes passed. Then a shout went up: "The northeast sky!" Everyone looked in that direction. A bright streak flashed across the heavens and disappeared down behind the rim of the cliff. The Wondrous Star had picked up the soul of Ancientone.

The Mumwalds rolled onto their feet. They jumped and shouted in joy. Some danced in little circles, their arms waving wildly. Others snapped their fingers and did as much of a jig as their webbed feet would allow. The oldest female Mumwald was safely on her journey to the Land Beyond. And the star had come on the very night of the ceremony! It was a good sign—Great Maker was watching over them closely. Usually they had to take turns keeping watch for several nights before the star was spotted. Sometimes what they dreaded most happened: the star didn't come at all in ten nights. If that did happen, the soul of the dead was reckoned to be lost, carried to No Place by the cold North Wind. They would never meet up with it in the blessed Land Beyond.

But this time all was well. At Sage's signal, the whole group hurried to the lakeshore, where Ancientone's body had been placed. Captain and Strongheart, a particularly worthy male, gently lifted the body into the water. Then they waded in themselves and began towing it toward the falls. When they got close enough to feel the slightest tug of current, they released the body and stroked their way slowly back toward the shore. Ancientone's remains melted into the darkness, to be carried over the falls and out of the valley.

In spite of the death, the spirits of the Mumwalds were high because of the quick coming of the star. Sage passed the word that they would have a meeting in the theater the next day to discuss what to do next.

5

Troubling Questions

The next morning, by the time the sun had arisen far enough to brighten the western shore of the lake, every Mumwald was once again congregated in the theater. Though a slight pall of sadness was apparent among the crowd now, spirits were still basically up. Lazy and Strongheart were chatting before Sage opened the proceedings.

"I'll bet Sage has a plan that will take care of this orange spot business in no time," said Strongheart.

"Well, I suppose he does," said Lazy, "but I do hope the labor involved isn't too heavy."

Jester overheard this last remark and broke in. "My, my, Lazy, and to think, when you were still just a few days old, one of the names your mother was considering for you was Chipper. Now wouldn't that have—"

At that moment Captain clicked two stones together to get everyone's attention. The assembly quickly quieted and everybody looked down at Sage, who had obviously worked himself into a positive mood for this gathering. He spoke in a kindly yet firm voice.

"As you know, yesterday brought a degree of unpleasantness into our midst. Above all, we lost our beloved sister, Ancientone. She will be sorely missed. However, she lived a normal lifespan for a Mumwald, and she filled that lifespan with good deeds and a cheerful demeanor. In accord with Great Maker's infinitely wise plan, it was indeed time for her to make way for a young Mumwald to bring new energy and a new perspective into our collective life. Thus, though we mourn our loss, we look to that which rises out of the perishing. We await with eagerness the birth of Motherfive's baby. And we continue to rejoice that Ancientone has passed quickly to the Land Beyond. We look forward to the time when we will be reunited with her there.

"Let us now turn our attention to a matter of importance for our future. Probably all of you have heard by now that the last cone that Climber threw down was blighted by the orange disease. It is now clear that it wasn't some kind of ground fungus just starting to spread upward when we discovered it. Cones anywhere on the trees may be infected, so we can't hope to control the problem by picking and discarding diseased cones from the low branches within our reach. It seems to me we have several...uh, Motherone, did you wish to interrupt?" His eyelids dipped almost imperceptibly in the slightest of frowns.

"Yes...yes...I feel I must...but I apologize...it's just that...well, you seemed to be ignoring...you see, I...."

"Please, Motherone, come out with it so that we may get back to the task at hand."

Stargazer spoke up. "I believe I can help. Last night after the ceremony and after Motherone had put Climber to bed, she came to me with troubling questions. Perhaps I should say it was a troubling feeling, for she had difficulty putting it into questions. We spent a long time trying to formulate exactly what she was getting at. I think it is a matter that should be brought before the whole group."

Sage was still mildly irritated, but he realized that he needed to deal with this new problem before the combined energy of all the Mumwalds could be focused on the cone situation. He looked from Stargazer to Motherone and then back to Stargazer. "Proceed, whoever wishes to bring the questions before us."

Stargazer nodded encouragingly to Motherone. The hesitant mother felt the warm spot on her side where Climber cuddled close to her. She breathed deeply and spoke rapidly but with conviction. "I won't waste words this time. What it all comes down to is, I don't understand what is happening to our lives. Yesterday we had three frightening experiences.

We discovered a possibly serious problem with our food supply. Then Climber almost got carried away by that dreadful eagle. And finally, Ancientone died. We have been taught how to deal with the death of an old one. We can accept that. But what about these other two terrible threats? How do we explain them? Why have they happened?"

She stopped abruptly after the burst of questions. Not a Mumwald peeped, not even Sage. Most of the Mumwalds were totally unused to thinking about such weighty concerns. Their lives had floated along so smoothly for so many generations that they hadn't had any stimulus to entertain questions such as Motherone was raising. Sage himself had very rarely

pondered such matters since the time of his instruction for becoming a sage. He felt very uneasy as his memory began a search for answers.

Stargazer was different. He was just entering his instruction. His mind was being introduced to a host of ideas that had never occurred to him and he was actively engaged in trying to put these ideas together into a meaningful whole. Sage, the instructor, was the source of these ideas, of course, but Sage had long since passed the time when his mind actively processed the thoughts. Furthermore, Stargazer had a naturally more meditative disposition than Sage. Sage had the necessary practical wisdom and skill in manipulating interpersonal relationships to keep the little society running smoothly in good times. His capacity to handle troublesome times had never been tested.

Stargazer was the first to speak after Motherone quit. "We have been brought up to believe that our lives will go well so long as we follow certain simple procedures. Now our lives suddenly face disruption from more than one source. Does this mean our belief is wrong, or does it mean that we have veered away from proper procedures?"

"Yup, I get it," said Dumbell. "I'll bet we've been bad—really bad. Yup, I'll bet we have." He laughed hoarsely and looked around with another knowing grin on his face. "And we didn't even know it! Yup, that's a real laugher!"

"Well, I don't get it," grumbled Muscles. "Can't we get this over with and get back to the important stuff?"

"Muscles," said Sage, adopting now a conciliatory tone, "I know that you and others prefer action over words, but we do have a concern here that must be dealt with. We ask for your patience—and your input, if something comes to your mind.

"Now, let us return to the, uh, questions that Motherone and Stargazer have brought up." The confidence had left Sage's voice. He was unsure what to say next. As he had been talking, he had been continuing to dredge his memory for help. All he had come up with was a series of statements—almost a litany—that kept repeating itself in the back of his mind: "Sin is dead. The word *sin* has been purged from our language. The idea of sin is no longer needed to explain our existence. Sin is dead." He recognized that this litany was relevant to the situation at hand, but he was fearful about bringing it into the open. Sages of long ago must have had good reason to drop the idea of sin. What would be the consequences of reinstating it into the thought processes of all the Mumwalds?

"Sage?" asked Stargazer quietly. "Are you all right?"

"Uh, oh—why, yes, of course, my son. These are heavy matters and I was trying to decide which way to proceed."

"What does the wisdom of the ages tell you?"

Sage couldn't bring himself to answer the question directly. "It, ah, it says that Mumwalds no longer need to trouble themselves with some of the ideas that might be used to answer your questions."

"That's good enough for me," said Muscles. He looked around at others for support. "Come on! You all heard Sage. We're not supposed to be talking about whatever it is we're talking about." Motherfour, sitting next to Muscles, eased her hand over to touch the indignant Mumwald. He acknowledged the touch with a slight turn of his sphere toward his favorite female. The other Mumwalds stared either downward at the ledges or off into the forest. Two or three shuffled uneasily on their seats.

Motherone, her thumb nervously stroking Climber's fur, finally said, "Sage, these questions will not die. They will keep festering in our minds and become sore spots unless they are tended to—now."

"But Motherone," the old leader said cautiously, "the events that stimulated these thoughts only happened yesterday. Don't you think if you let more time pass, the questions too will pass? Shouldn't we set them aside for now and see if they are still pressing within us in, say, seven days?"

Motherone shook her sphere, not in anger but with great solemnity. Sage looked at Stargazer, who stared straight into Sage's eyes and shook his sphere too. Sage knew that he could make the decision to ignore the questions and order the proceedings to return to the subject of the diseased cones. No Mumwald would argue further with him if they saw that his mind was made up. They would all, in fact, try their best to comply with his command and focus on the food problem. But he knew also that in the quiet darkness of night, when each Mumwald was most alone and pressures from outside each Mumwald were weakest, mysterious forces would be stirring deep inside the more restive of the spirits among them. Mumwalds were not mere puppets, following their leader blindly without an act of willing. Mumwald society worked because each individual Mumwald wanted it to work and thought that its proper working was in the best interest of the individual. If he didn't deal now with Motherone's feelings, he knew that they would indeed pop out again, perhaps in even more disruptive ways.

All eyes were anxiously watching Sage ruminate. Finally, without even glancing over toward Muscles, Sage raised his sphere to gaze at the massive cliff wall behind the gathering. "Let us discuss the questions further," he said firmly. "Who would speak first?"

"Bah!" said Muscles immediately, squirming in his seat.

"We need your guidance, Sage," said Stargazer. "Have we in some way—no matter how seemingly insignificant—been violating the way the wisdom of the ages deems it best that we behave?"

"We sure have," said Sneaky. "I can answer that one. We got careless when we let Climber be exposed to the eagle. That was a no-no for sure."

Sage nodded gravely in agreement. "True, true. And that bit of carelessness indirectly led to the death of Ancientone. Yet it was time for her to die, as we have said. And Climber is safely in the arms of Motherone now. Neither one of these events vexes me. The cone problem does. The carelessness of today couldn't have caused that."

"Yes," said Strongheart, "I see what you mean. There is no right time to have a cone problem, so we can't dismiss it as one of those things whose time has come. Nor is it a threat that will just go away, as the eagle did. And yet I don't see what we have done wrong that has led to this threat."

"Well now, my children. I am impressed with your discussion. I didn't realize such clear thinking would come out of so many of your minds." As he spoke, Sage was beginning to feel better. Perhaps he wouldn't have to reinstate the idea of sin after all if it wasn't relevant to the situation.

Motherone couldn't let the matter rest, however. "But Sage, think deeply. We *must* be doing something against the received wisdom. Perhaps it is something none of us are aware of." Her face paled as another thought came to her mind. She barely whispered it. "Perhaps not even you know of the wrong that we unwittingly do."

Stargazer was following closely. "Maybe...maybe it is something we don't have any control over, some way of doing things that we are born with and take completely for granted."

A shudder visibly shook Sage. His memory had been jogged again. It was reaching now further back, behind the sin litany to another thought associated with sin. Far, far back in time, when early sages had struggled to explain the happenings of the world to themselves and their fellow Mumwalds, they had entertained a certain idea for a lengthy period of time. They had called the idea "born-in-sinfulness." It was assumed that every Mumwald had been born with a flaw in his or her developing soul, a flaw that could never be totally purged from the soul no matter how hard an individual tried. Slowly, ever so slowly, however, over a period of hundreds of generations Mumwalds learned how to fine-tune their behavior and their attitudes and the way they nurtured their young. First there began to appear an occasional Mumwald who lived such a blessed and beatific life that others thought surely he or she had somehow escaped or overcome the born-in-sinfulness curse. Gradually, more and more Mumwalds achieved this state of being. And so, long before the idea of sin itself was dropped, the idea of born-in-sinfulness was banished from thought, except as it was retained in the tradition passed on only to sages.

This time Mothersix expressed the concern everyone felt as they watched their venerable leader struggle inwardly. "Sage, perhaps it would help you—and us—if you would share your thoughts."

"Oh, I don't know, good mother, I just don't know. I am in a quandary precisely over the question of whether to share certain thoughts with you."

"Do it, Sage," said Stargazer simply.

Sage was almost amused by his understudy, always eager for the next lesson. "Very well, my children. Listen carefully and you shall hear words spoken only between sages for generations upon generations. Don't be quick to judge either the merits of the ideas or the decisions to hold them from you." With that preamble, Sage launched into a discussion of sin, beginning with the Mumwalds' definition of the word. For most Mumwalds it had meant something one Mumwald did that made another suffer, either mentally, physically, emotionally, or spiritually. He told how, in the early days of their society, Mumwalds had stolen from each other and lied to each other and even killed each other. He almost mentioned rape, for that too had been a reality among them, but he shied away from it at the last moment. From his own inner experience, he knew that Mumwalds still had sexual urges toward members of the opposite sex other than selected partners. But he knew also that their highly developed nurturing methods had successfully restricted the outlet for these urges to the realm of completely private fantasy. There were no macho locker room stories or titillating ladies room chatter in Mumwalds' lives—and not because locker rooms and ladies rooms did not exist. To mention rape openly would be to violate this most carefully developed status, and he did not feel the subject was needed to illustrate sin.

"So what does this idea of sin have to do with anything?" said Muscles huffily.

"Muscles, you are exasperating," said Motherone. "Can't you see that Sage is going to use this idea of sin to help explain what is happening to us?"

"Yup, I told you! I told you we had done a biggie. I'll bet we're the best sinners there ever was. That's why we're being punished with them orange painted cones. Yup, it's as simple as that." As usual, Dumbell was, in his own distinctive manner, expressing thoughts that were running through many of the Mumwalds' minds.

"If what Dumbell says is true," asked Mothersix, "then who or what is doing the punishing?" Then a thought struck her. "Oh my!...No, it couldn't...could it be?..." She looked quizzically at Sage.

Sage nodded his sphere. "I think you suspect the answer that the sages of old would have given. In the old days, they believed that when we sinned we were punished by Great Maker, just as a mother Mumwald holds her child upside down when the child errs."

The Mumwalds sat stunned. Once a month, at full moon, they gathered either at the lakeshore or in the theater and held a brief ceremony to acknowledge their dependence on Great Maker for creating and maintaining their tidy little world. The dominant note of the ceremony was praise for Great Maker's wisdom and goodness in allowing and aiding such a place to develop. Suddenly to introduce the idea that this superior being might have a dark side, an angry side, a punitive side, was a shock.

Sage understood the mood that pervaded his audience. "Now, now, my children, you must remember that these ideas that we are introducing are no longer believed to be true. I brought up sin so that we could discuss Motherone's questions. She wondered if we, or at least one of us, had done something wrong to bring down troubles upon us. In other words, she wondered if we had sinned. I did not bring up this idea in order to say that it is true, for my analysis of the situation has not revealed any significant sin among us. We were a bit careless with Climber, true. But sin? No, not there—or anywhere else in our lives that I can see. Therefore, it is irrelevant to concern ourselves with old ideas attached to Great Maker also. There is no reason for us to change our picture of Him. He is still the wise, all-powerful father who has brought us and our world into existence, and He is the one who generously maintains the necessities for our continuing existence." It made Sage feel good to get on a positive note, to affirm long-held beliefs that supported the society's happy life. "I hope that these reminders bring comfort to you and satisfy the questioning that is going on in some of your minds." He smiled benignly at his listeners.

"Brother, so do I!" blurted Muscles. He slapped his hands against his legs in the Mumwald way of clapping. A few others followed suit.

"But Sage," said Stargazer, "you haven't exactly spoken to my conjecture that our problems are caused by a kind of inborn sinfulness, some kind of action we take that causes suffering even though we don't consciously intend that result."

Sage was amazed at his pupil. He was going to be a great one, this Stargazer. He had nearly come up with the phrase "born-in-sinfulness" all on his own, and he had certainly generated the basic idea in his own mind without the direct input of the ancient wisdom. But Sage was also just a little put out, for the youth was forcing the elder's hand again, compelling him to reveal even more of the ancient thinking. Sage sighed visibly and then reluctantly explained the meaning of born-in-sinfulness and the reason for its dismissal from active use as a concept. "You see," he said, trying to end the discussion for good, "we have now lived too many generations without any serious problems that could be attributed to born-in-sinfulness. It is not reasonable to think that we could suddenly revert to such a condition. I assure you, loved ones, I have thought deeply about our situation and I find nothing in our actions, thought, or beliefs that could be interpreted as a cause for the unfortunate happenings." He paused to take stock of the mood of his listeners. Climber and Mischief were fast asleep beside their mothers. Other young were fiddling with sticks or pebbles. Most of the adults were staring into the distance with unfocused eyes and expressionless mouths. Only Motherone and Stargazer on the one side and Muscles on the other gazed intently at the speaker.

It was time, in Sage's judgment, to close the discussion. "Now that we have dealt with questions of cause," he continued firmly, "we must get back to this aggravating cone problem. However, since our mental energy has surely been depleted by our discussion, we need a recess. We will meet again when the shadow of the western cliff strikes the westernmost point of the lake. You are dismissed—oh, and remember to eat only the cones in storage in our caves."

6

Questions Persist

Released from the somber proceedings, most Mumwalds hurriedly left the theater and headed for a swim in the cool, refreshing lake water. The sun was past mid-morning. Tiny white puffs of clouds dotted the sky in the west, but none shielded the valley. The ledges of the theater were no place to spend long periods of time in the searing, dry heat of the bright summer sun. Even Sage admitted paddling lazily about in the water would be most welcome. Only Motherone and Stargazer remained at their seats. Mothersix had sensed Motherone's continuing agitated state and had offered to look after Climber for a while.

Motherone stared down at the gray rock ledge at her feet and slowly let her fingers stroke circles in the warm rock at her sides. Stargazer shoved himself off the ledge and stretched his arms and legs. When the last of the other Mumwalds were far into the meadow and out of earshot, Motherone spoke, a touch of bitterness in her low voice. "He didn't answer the questions of cause at all."

Stargazer put all his weight on one webbed foot and kicked gently at a loose stone with the other. "He tried, the best way he knew how."

"But it didn't do any good. He just tried to say what the cause wasn't. And he used stale, old ideas to do that! He never did even try to get at what the cause *is*."

"Yes, yes. I don't think he even realized that's how he ended things. Give him a chance. It's only reasonable that he would rely on the tradition given to us by Great Maker. No sage has had to tackle questions like these in many years. He just doesn't—"

"I wish you were the sage right now."

"Now, now, I have only begun my instruction the last few months, and I have yet to hear much of the received wisdom. Just take those ideas of sin and born-in-sinfulness. Fascinating. Maybe they are stale and old, as you say, but still they open up so many new avenues of thought. I hope we continue to—"

"You would know how to explore my questions with the whole group. You wouldn't be afraid to raise doubts about pronouncements from the past." Motherone had lifted her gaze now and was staring straight into the forest. "You at least would understand the questions, where they are coming from, why they must be confronted. Sage dealt with them because he thought it was politically wise, not because he felt any basic sympathy with them. He is too shallow a person to deal adequately with what we are facing, Stargazer."

Stargazer didn't know what to say. He felt great loyalty and friendship toward Sage. He would be the last person to support a change in leadership. Besides, such changes were out of the question in the Mumwald scheme of things. They would mark disorder in the ranks, pitting Mumwald against Mumwald. Harmony would be destroyed. Someone would suffer painful feelings of rejection.

As these ideas unfolded quickly in Stargazer's mind, the word *sin* suddenly popped up again. He wondered if competing for the office of sage would be considered sin. Motherone was opening up one troubling question after another. And yet, Stargazer sensed with discomfort that she was right about Sage. "Let's take a walk along the forest path, where we won't be bothered," he said finally.

Motherone slid off the ledge and followed Stargazer as he padded toward the canopy of trees. Once they had both entered the shadowy, scented pathway, he stopped to let her catch up. He clasped her right hand in his left and intertwined his fingers with hers—in so far as such pudgy fingers could intertwine.

"You have been badly shaken," he began. "Your questions deserve an attempt at a full and complete answer. Rather than blame someone else for not coming up with the answer, let's work on it ourselves—just the two of us here. Perhaps we have as good a chance as anyone of finding a satisfying answer."

Motherone squeezed his hand. "Thank you, Stargazer."

They walked on in silence. A piping peep pierced the air. Stargazer released his hand from Motherone's and knelt on both knees, holding out both hands, palms up, toward the cliff side of the path. Moments later they heard a rustling sound at the base of the nearest spruce. A little chipmunk head darted up from behind a big root. For several seconds its nose twitched and its round, dark eyes stared. Satisfied, it scooted out into the path and up to Stargazer's outreaching hands. The Mumwald had nothing to feed it but softly stroked its back. Then, just as suddenly as it had announced itself, it scurried off into the needle-packed forest floor.

Stargazer twisted his sphere to look up at Motherone. "Do you suppose his world has changed as drastically as ours has in the last day or so?"

Motherone chuckled. "It wouldn't appear so."

Stargazer remained on his knees. "What do you suppose a chipmunk would think if an eagle carried off its mate or a rock slide buried one of its young?"

"Chipmunks don't think, silly."

"But they seem to have some kind of conscious awareness of what is going on. They must think in some sense or other."

"It isn't thinking. They just accept what happens. Like we accept the death of Ancientone. It's the way things are and there's no use worrying about it."

"Should we not then learn a lesson from them?"

"What do you mean?"

"We know how to accept a timely death of an ancientone, but we can't accept the untimely death of Climber at the talons of an eagle or the premature death of many Mumwalds due to starvation. Maybe these kinds of events are just part of the natural way things happen. Should we not embark on a program to nurture an attitude of acceptance toward all such events?"

"Heavens, no! That would be insensitive. We can't deny the feelings of sorrow and fear we have at untimely deaths. We're built differently from the chipmunks."

"Hmmm. I wonder."

Stargazer rose from his knees, reached for Motherone's hand, and led her on down the path.

"You see," said Motherone, "that's what I mean."

"Huh?"

"Your mind just naturally likes to explore ideas that are suggested to you by very ordinary occurrences. You can see how different bits of our experience relate to each other. You lead others to think through things. You don't just try to supply answers from the past to get others to shut up. You'd be a great sage for now."

Stargazer blushed. "I'm not sure our discussion about chipmunks was all that useful."

"Who knows? As we reflect on it, maybe something else will occur to one of us. But the point is, your attitude and method of inquiry is what we need now, not Sage's grudging acknowledgment of a problem and his attempts to find perfunctory answers."

"Muscles wouldn't agree with you."

"Bosh on Muscles!"

"We're definitely in the minority, you know. Most of our fellow Mumwalds are more like Muscles but are too nice to say so."

"I don't care. Come on! I feel much better now! Let's join the others!" With that, Motherone thumped into the lead, jerked Stargazer's arm, and led him off the path straight through the forest toward the lake. Squeals of delight and merry splashing noises grew louder and louder as they twisted their way through the tightly knit trees. When patches of the beautiful blue water came into view through the trees, they stopped to watch. One group of floating Mumwalds, both young and adult, had formed a circle and were gleefully raking water with their fingers, flinging sprays at each other. Several Mumwalds lazily paddled close to shore, while a few sat on flat rocks that dotted the bank and dangled their webbed feet in the cooling water.

Stargazer started to move out of the trees to join the bathers, but Motherone tugged at his arm. He turned to face her, puzzled. She held out her free hand. He raised his into her grasp. Their faces were very close. She leaned forward so that her little pebble nose gently touched his. Then, with her nose still against his, she slightly tilted her sphere backwards and pushed forwards with open mouth. Her lips encircled his closed mouth. Her tongue slid back and forth across his closed lips. He shuddered and closed his eyes. She pulled back and whispered, "I'm so proud that you are Climber's father." Then, hand in hand, they burst out of the trees and practically tumbled face first into the waiting water.

7

A Startling Revelation

age watched contentedly as the Mumwalds enjoyed themselves under the balming influence of the lake. He had not spent long in the cold water, for he had found it stiffened his leg joints. He was propped comfortably against the smooth surface of a large, rounded boulder at the edge of the water. Suddenly he saw a cloud shadow moving rapidly toward him from the western shore of the lake. He looked to the sky. Those earlier puffs of cloud had assembled into massive, billowing thunderheads, one of which was dominating the western sky. A low rumble of thunder rolled into the valley.

Sage picked up two small stones and clacked them together several times. "Come, my children, gather around me here. Out of the lake! Off your fannies! Join me quickly!"

The Mumwalds obediently splashed out of the water and formed a semicircle in front of Sage, who remained resting against his boulder. "The weather is unpredictable," Sage began, "and who knows what it will be like at the appointed time for our gathering. I've decided to go ahead here and now, for I have truly exciting things to reveal to you and I would not be able to stand waiting until tomorrow to tell you." The calmness in his eyes and his relaxed posture did not fit the exhilaration in his voice, but the crowd properly took their cue from the voice. Fists were clenched in anticipation, and more than one youngster had his or her hand squeezed too tightly by an excited parent. A lightning bolt snapped down at the cliff top, and a shattering crack of thunder ripped over their heads.

"I must hurry," said Sage, and with that he swiftly outlined a plan he had devised as the next step in dealing with the cone problem. The Mumwalds uttered many "Oooohs!" and "Aaaahs!" and remarks like "I didn't know that!" as they listened. Large drops of rain splatted down just as he finished his explanation. The whole company retreated to their caves as quickly as they could waddle, their imaginations fired to great heights by Sage's words.

Fortunately, the storm was short-lived. Captain, who had taken shelter in Sage's cave, peered straight up the cliff from the cave mouth and said, "Blue sky directly above us, Sage. The rest of the afternoon may be decent."

"Good. Let's begin your adventure. Go get the others."

By "others" Sage meant specifically Strongheart and Muscles, but as soon as Captain and those two were spotted marching past other caves, the entire tribe appeared outside Sage's home. Sage had appointed the three males to be a scouting party. He had told the Mumwalds of an old legend that talked about a secret passage thought to lead out of the valley. The legend was, of course, part of the received wisdom and was to be revealed only in case of emergency. Sage felt that the cone crisis was such a case. If the scouts did get out of the valley, they might find trees whose cones were untainted by the blight, thus bringing a quick, easy close to the problem—and hopefully to the dreaded questions that erupted out of the situation.

Sage led the throng back along the lake path. Almost everyone was jabbering or croaking excitedly. The tops of the three scouts' bodies tingled and their arms and legs were taut with nervous energy. Sneaky was in an especially playful mood. He snuck up behind Motherfive and pinched her on the back.

"Ouch!" she cried. "Sneaky, why did you do that?"

"Just wanted to see if you were awake, my love."

"You'll know I'm awake if you try that again! And watch when you call me 'my love'!"

The Mumwalds croaked gaily.

Even the young ones had caught the excitement. Rammer and Roller, Motherthree's twins, were having a ball. Over and over they played their favorite game. Rammer bent over forward so that his forehead stuck out farther than his nose. Then he ran as fast as he could at the back of Roller, who was loping more slowly in the same direction. As Rammer rushed up behind his brother, he gave him a mighty upward and forward boost with his hands and forehead. At the instant Roller's feet left the ground, he curled up his arms and legs and closed his eyes. When he came down, he was nearly a perfect ball and rolled and rolled and rolled along the path. After he finally stopped, he clambered to his feet laughing and prepared for the next ramming shove from his brother.

There was more to everyone's feelings than excitement, of course. Not even Sage knew for sure when or if a Mumwald had ever actually left the valley and come back. No wonder each person felt an odd mixture of fear and hope and gaiety and awe.

Sage turned off the path as it left the lake. He led the way along the lakeshore and across the meadow toward the southern cliff, finally halting at a wheel-sized stone at the base of the sheer wall.

"You see this large stone that seems to lean slightly against the cliff?" he said.

"Yes," said Captain.

"What about it?" said Muscles.

"Righto, my good man," said Dumbell.

"Behind that stone is supposed to be the entrance to the passage," continued Sage. "I've never see it, of course. As I have said, the legend does not say for sure where the passage leads. Before you enter, let me repeat a part of the legend word for word so you will know what I know." He paused to clear his throat. A faraway look came to his eyes as he began.

Out of light,
Into dark,
Down through darkness we went.

Slowly we walked,
Feeling our way,
Into darkness we crept.

Pounding, throbbing,
Fear in each sphere,
Eyes on darkness were set.

Swooshing, roaring,
Rushed to our ears,
Sound in darkness we met.

Slippery, slimy,
Hands felt the rock,
Walls in darkness were wet.

Pounding, throbbing,
Fear in each sphere,
Out of darkness we leapt!

"Do you see what this means?" asked Sage. And before Dumbell, or anyone else for that matter, could answer, he went on. "These early explorers seem to have found that the passage went downward toward the bottom of the waterfall. However, they became frightened by the loud noise and wetness and came back before they had gone all the way." He paused to look at the three scouts, hoping they weren't getting spooked.

"I'm ready to start," said Strongheart in a solid, confident tone.

"You lead on from here, Captain," said Sage, smiling at Strongheart.

Captain strode up to the circular boulder. "First, move the stone," he ordered. Several males pushed against one side of the big rock with all their might, trying to roll it away from the supposed entrance. It didn't budge. As they kept

straining against the rock, three of the females went back to the forest and returned with a long, thick stick. With some of the Mumwalds using the stick as a lever and others pushing with their hands, the stone slowly rolled to the side. Sure enough, a dark hole appeared in the cliff base. Everyone crowded around to peer into it. Their eyes were used to the bright sunlight. They could only see a few feet into the passage. Its ragged walls seemed just far enough apart to allow one full grown Mumwald to walk through without scraping his arms. The arched top gave plenty of clearance for the short creatures.

"Good luck!"

"Be careful!"

"Come back by sundown!"

Grumpy Muscles stepped over to Motherfour and touched his nose to hers, but didn't proceed with the rest of a Mumwald kiss, for it was strictly forbidden in public.

The three brave adventurers waved one last time, then filed into the darkness. Captain was in the lead, Strongheart in the rear. They had only gone a few feet when Captain stopped abruptly. Muscles bumped his nose into Captain's back, and Strongheart jammed into Muscles.

"A fine start," grumbled Muscles.

"We've got to wait for our eyes to get used to the dark," said Captain. He wiped his hand along the hard, uneven wall at his side. His nose twitched at the musty odor, but otherwise the air supply seemed satisfactory. Soon they could see much better. To their surprise, the passage seemed to end only ten paces ahead of them. They pushed ahead to the end wall. Solid rock enclosed them on three sides and at their feet.

"We might as well go back," said Muscles. "I didn't think this would go anywhere."

"Wait!" said Strongheart. "The fur on the top of my sphere feels funny. It's being...air flowing! My fur is waving slightly in a little breeze."

"You're right," said Captain, sensing the air on his top. "The passage must go on." Stretching to the limit on the tips of his webbed feet, he began feeling up high along the wall where very little light reached. "Here! It feels like an open space. And it's in the direction of the falls. Take my basket, Strongheart. Now, Muscles, boost me up."

The strongest of the Mumwalds squatted and slid his hands under Captain. With a mighty grunt, he hoisted his leader up to the height of his top. Captain half rolled and half crawled into the opening. It was very dark up there. He felt around. Ahead of him the passage seemed about the same size as the one below, but right here at the opening it was double width. He turned back and, speaking softly, told Strongheart to hand up the basket. Then, with Strongheart shoving from below and Captain pulling from above, heavy Muscles made it up. He rolled onto his face and scooted out over the edge, with Captain holding his legs. Muscles reached down and grabbed both of Strongheart's outstretched hands, dragging him up and scraping his nose in the process.

"Humph," said Strongheart, "now I'll be accused of finding and rubbing noses with so many females that my nose turned red!" Even Muscles couldn't suppress a chuckle at that.

Once on the shelf the three inched forward. The darkness was total now, but the passage was still narrow enough to let them feel both sides. Captain stopped once to wonder aloud, "I don't understand why the passage is so straight and almost the same size all the way."

"And the path is so smooth," added Strongheart. "I've heard Sage tell that our legends say our ancestors hollowed out our home caves. Perhaps the same craftsmen carved out this passage."

"Perhaps," said Captain. "But the explorers Sage just talked about didn't even go all the way to the falls. You would think if they knew where…."

"Hey, can we get on with it?" growled Muscles. "It's creepy in here."

The passage was level for several more steps, then Captain's webbed feet suddenly felt the path slope steeply downward. He began sliding each foot in front of the other, as he leaned backward. He didn't want to trip or lose his balance, for he doubted if there was any way to stop a rolling Mumwald on that incline. Soon a faint rumbling sound came to them. It gradually grew louder.

"That's the roar and the swoosh that the legend spoke of," whispered Strongheart.

A moment later Captain jerked his hand away from the wall. "Yiii! I just touched some slimy stuff."

"Ugh, this cool mist gives me the chills," mumbled Muscles. Shortly, the walls became dripping wet.

Captain reached a point where the path once again leveled off. Ahead he saw faint, diffused light. He turned around to tell the others but realized the thundering of the falls was too loud to allow talking in anything but a shout. And he was afraid to yell. As the exit to the passage shone before him, the threat of the unknown beyond closed in on him. He wanted silence. He would let the others discover the light for themselves.

8

An Irritated Sage

Back in the Mumwalds' valley the crowd around the passage entrance quietly dispersed once the explorers were on the ledge and out of earshot. It would be a long afternoon of waiting.

Stargazer ambled up to Sage and said, "I think we'd better talk."

"Certainly, my son. Where?"

Stargazer pointed to a shady spot under a large spruce at the edge of the forest. When they reached it, they eased themselves down to sit on the thick, spongy bed of needles, each leaning against the massive trunk. They weren't facing each other in these positions, but these two were close enough friends that they didn't need to watch each other in order to communicate fully and directly and honestly. For several minutes they sat in silence, watching other Mumwalds. Healer was moseying about the meadow. Occasionally she stooped to pick a particular herb or other plant for her medicine basket. Lazy was lying on his back in a bed of damp, cool grass by the lakeshore. Climber, Mischief, Rammer, Roller, and Punky were playing keep away out on the lake with a small stick. Mischief wailed, "You big guys never let me catch it!"

Eventually, Stargazer sighed deeply, feeling he had to start the conversation despite dreading to do so. "Sage, I hesitate to bring it up, but I think we have a problem."

"I know that, my son—we do have a problem. What bothers you about discussing it?"

"I don't think we're talking about the same problem."

"Oh?"

"You were thinking of the cone problem, weren't you?"

Sage nodded as he said, "Of course."

"Well, I'm talking about a problem related to the questions that were discussed in the gathering this morning."

"Oh, did you think it was not right of me to reveal the ideas of sin and born-in-sinfulness?"

"No, no, I'm quite glad you did that. Very stimulating—at least for some of us. You see, that's the problem. A few of us have dispositions very different from the majority. We enjoy receiving new ideas and trying to fit them in to our way of thinking about our experiences. We like to expand our thought horizons, to venture into new areas. More than that, we feel a need to question, to ask why things are happening the way they are. Normally we few do this in private conversations— of course, you know this because I've reported several of them to you. And you've always said that a little idle speculation can do no harm. Now, though, the frightening experiences of yesterday have stirred strong, deep feelings that have attached themselves to certain questions. Do you see what I'm driving at?"

"Certainly," said Sage, a hint of irritation in his voice. "So Motherone is still upset? I thought I had quieted her fears this morning."

Stargazer scooped up a handful of spruce needles and rubbed them between his two open hands. "Please don't be angry with her. She isn't the only one with questions, but Climber's near loss did move her powerfully. I'm afraid your answers this morning didn't satisfy several of us." Stargazer was fudging here, for he actually knew of no one else other than Motherone and himself who was disturbed. He was relying on his knowledge of other Mumwalds to guess that at least a couple more shared the questioning attitude.

"I don't see what more I could have said."

"Perhaps nothing. But we still don't have a clue about why these incidents happened yesterday. All you told us is they aren't some kind of payback for sin, nor are they the result of a faulty Mumwald nature. What is the cause then?"

Sage stirred on his cushion of needles. "I'm not sure I see the need to try to answer that question. Great Maker has created us and set us up to live under certain conditions. So long as we aren't responsible for fouling up the works, I don't see that we have anything to worry about. We should simply accept the way things are, play by the rules that have gotten us this far, and take what comes. What more can we do?"

"Hmmm. I'm not sure I like what your attitude implies about Great Maker. Aren't we supposed to believe that He cares about us personally?"

"Certainly, and He does, I assure you."

"And isn't He supposed to have control over everything that happens?"

"Of course, down to the minutest detail if He chooses to control to that extent." Sage was simply reacting with answers born of the knowledge he had received. His tone was matter-of-fact. He obviously was not actively engaging these questions, nor did he see where the sequence of questions was leading.

Stargazer was disappointed at the aloofness of Sage. He had thought the old leader would begin to empathize with the questioners once he was confronted with certain paths of thought. The young Mumwald reached out and grabbed his own webbed feet in his hands. Very slowly he rocked forward and backward, attempting to quell his negative feelings toward his beloved mentor. After several moments he felt he could continue in a calm tone. "Doesn't it bother you that our all-powerful, caring Supreme Being would let bad things happen to us?"

"Ah, my son, is that what is bothering you? In your pride you have forgotten one of the most fundamental facts of our condition. We are very limited in our understanding of the way our world works and why it works that way. We always have been and we will always be. That is why we aren't supreme beings. You must not let your pride in the power of your mind force you to go beyond where you can reasonably be expected to go."

"But I don't see that my question takes us beyond where we should go. I'm not sure the received wisdom is adequate to guide us at this point."

At this, Sage rotated on his bottom so that he could look straight at this upstart young Mumwald beside him. Stargazer did not turn to meet the fierce stare. "What did you say?" Sage said, almost curtly.

"I...I said I'm not sure—"

"I heard what you said. And I am shocked. A sage in training has no right to doubt the received wisdom. There is a vast amount of knowledge I have not yet revealed to you. At least you could wait until your training is complete. You must exert patience beyond all else and not let your judgment fly off upon flimsy evidence."

Stargazer refused to be cowed. He kept looking straight out from the tree trunk as he spoke. "But I thought you had revealed to us the received wisdom that was pertinent to our questions. And that wisdom has failed to quiet our minds. Maybe...couldn't Great Maker be trying somehow to speak to us now outside the word of the tradition?"

Sage spoke directly into Stargazer's ear in a low, firm voice. "This discussion has gone on quite long enough. You need time to ponder my words before you make any further rash statements."

Stargazer reluctantly rose to his feet and took a step.

Sage suddenly raised a hand and said, "Stop. Help me up." Stargazer did as he was told.

"I can't let you leave this way," the elder Mumwald said. "Give me a rub."

Stargazer's eyes abruptly began filling with tears. He reached out his two hands and took Sage's, then tilted his sphere forward, as did Sage. The two foreheads met and moved slowly back and forth in a mutual massaging motion. Sage squeezed the younger one's hands. They broke apart. Stargazer turned and shuffled off.

Sage sat back down against the tree and watched his pupil go. He couldn't remember ever having spoken to a fellow Mumwald the way he had just done, except perhaps once or twice to Dumbell when that poor oaf was especially exasperating. Sage wondered aloud, "I wonder if we have descended back into a state of sin, for there is no doubt that Stargazer has just made me suffer uncommon anguish of heart, and I obviously have had the same effect on him. I must search my memory of the received wisdom. I can remember no teaching about the possibility of such a reversion." He shut his eyes and let his mind float free, hoping to have it run into something useful. Motherone had been keeping an eye on the pair sitting under the tree as she sat by the lake with other mothers. She could tell even from a distance that all was not going well. Healer came over to sit beside her. "You know," said the wise doctor-nurse, "I know what you're going through. Humph. Sage could learn a thing or two from my tradition." She spoke without malice.

"Hmm. Why don't you try to get through to the old fellow?"

"Now, now. You know that's strictly forbidden. The last time a healer tried to do that she was given the silent treatment by all the males for a whole moon cycle!" A sly grin stretched her lips. "We'll just keep our little tidbits of wisdom among us females, if you please."

"He probably has it all buried somewhere in his memory anyway and just doesn't want to let any of it out."

"No, no, I've told you before. We have much that he knows nothing about. Oh...Stargazer is breaking away from Sage."

Stargazer started walking through the meadow aimlessly toward the theater. He flattened a beautiful orange Indian paintbrush with a big webbed foot and brusquely brushed aside a tall gilia stem with its delicate red flowers that usually gave him such delight. Motherone asked Healer to keep an eye on Climber for a few minutes, then rose and headed toward him. He didn't notice her approach. As she caught up with him, she noticed the damp fur under his eyes and knew better than to say anything. They walked side by side without touching until they reached the theater. Stargazer clumsily climbed to the top ledge, turned, and sat with his back against the warm cliff. Motherone eased down beside him. The bright afternoon sun seemed to be making up for having been interrupted at its task by the earlier shower.

No sooner had she settled in for what she thought would be a long silence when he mumbled, "I don't like what is happening among us."

She reached out a hand, but he drew his away.

"I've just had the first truly unpleasant argument of my whole life, and who was it with? Sage! The one I most respect. What's going on?"

"You've argued with Muscles many times," Motherone said.

"Ah, yes, but we both know that we're just playing a game on the surface of things. We don't really care what the other is saying, for we know that we can go on living together no matter what each of us believes. But with Sage just now it was different. We differed, and it meant something very important. It touched feelings in me and in him that I would never have guessed existed. I thought Mumwalds held a fundamental commonness, a feeling bond, at the core of our beings—but now, I'm not so sure. I don't like this discovery at all."

Motherone's face tightened. "You didn't tell him that we had been discussing putting you in his place as sage, did you?"

"Ha. I wouldn't say we had been discussing that matter. You merely mentioned it, that's all. I didn't for a second seriously entertain the suggestion as a real possibility. And, no, I didn't mention it to him. Other things I said troubled him enough. But the fact that you proposed the idea with some seriousness bothers me. Think about it. Do you realize what we'd be doing if we actually tried to bring about such a change in leadership?"

"I'm not sure I know what you're getting at. But I don't much like the accusing tone you've been speaking in. You seem to think...."

Stargazer held up both hands to stop her. "Oh my," he said, this time in a conciliatory voice. "See how infectious all this is? First, we discuss virtual rebellion against our leader. Then I get him agitated and angry by pressing him for answers he does not have and therefore does not think are necessary. And now I strike at you with my tone of voice, unaware that I am doing it. Surely...surely...."

Motherone waited for him to go on. When he remained silent with his mouth wide open and his eyes staring blankly toward the western cliff rim, she spoke up. "Weren't you about to say, 'Surely we have been flirting dangerously with that state of sin that Sage told us about'?"

Tears once more squeezed out of his eyes. Motherone took his hand in hers again, and this time he did not pull away.

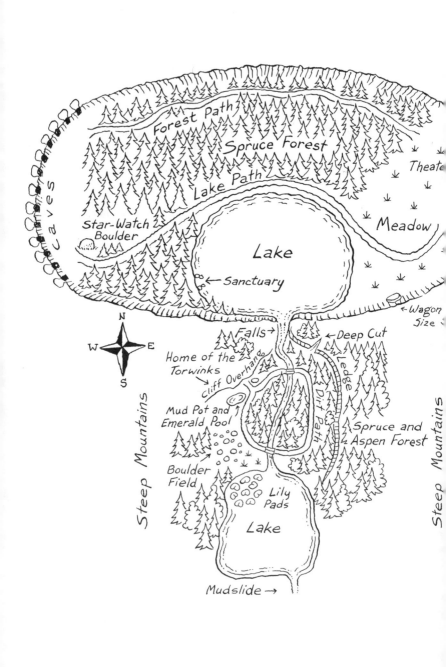

Forest Path

Spruce Forest

Lake Path

Theate

Caves

Star-Watch
Boulder

Lake

Meadow

← Sanctuary

N

W   E

S

Falls →

← Deep Cut

Wagon
Size

Home of the
Torwinks

Cliff Overhang

Deep Cut

Ledge

Dirt Path

Mud Pot and
Emerald Pool

Spruce and
Aspen Forest

Boulder
Field

Lily
Pads

Steep Mountains

Lake

Steep Mountains

Mudslide →

9

A Startling Discovery

Back in the passage in the southern cliff, the three scouts tiptoed their way toward the light that Captain had been the first to see. Soon the passage opened onto a ledge of rock behind the falls. Light flickered around them. Their downy white fur was made for water, yet they felt a cold chill as the mist and spray soaked them.

Through the thin curtain of falling water they could see the stream flowing gently away from the falls in a more or less straight line. Near the falls the stream was hemmed in by steep, slick walls of granite much like the cliffs of the Mumvald valley. But not more than twenty-five or thirty feet downstream, the steep walls seemed to fall rapidly away and the stream was lost to sight in a thick, dark forest.

The three looked at each other and then down at the bubling, swirling water six inches below them. Captain made a motion to show that they would have to jump in and float through the falls. Strongheart led the way without hesitation. The rough little waves kept pushing him back against the rock wall, but by thrusting hard with both his hands and his webbed feet, he worked his way forward. As he passed through the falls, he felt a light sting. Then the current caught him and ushered him on his way through the short canyon. Captain and Muscles quickly followed, using forceful strokes to push through the falls. They squinted. The light was extremely bright compared to the passage. They allowed the current to take hold of them, too, and they bobbed along not far behind Strongheart. Within seconds they were all swept abruptly into the semidarkness under the forest canopy where the valley began widening. They continued to float along as their eyes once again adjusted. The stream jogged suddenly to the left and then straightened out again. Right at that point a log lay clear across the stream, too low for them to pass under and too high to see over. Strongheart put out his arms to keep his nose from meeting the log. His companions veered to either side of him and came to rest against the log also.

"We'll have to get out and go around this," said Captain, pointing toward the right bank as the easiest exit from the water. Muscles was closest to that side and led the way. As he raised himself onto a rock clear of the water and looked ahead, he said, "Whoa! This isn't just any old fallen log. There are three others with it. They're held close together by these rocks on the bank."

The others joined him. Mumwalds had built similar bridges temporarily over spots in their own forest path that became boggy during the spring snow melt. Strongheart tapped the others on the arm and pointed down and back into the forest. A crude path ran off to the west. It was not cleaned and neatly outlined, as the Mumwald paths were, yet the dirt-needle mixture on its surface obviously had recently been stirred by something that made scratching marks.

Captain shrugged with his arms and then spoke softly so that his voice would blend with the muffled sound of the falls. "I wonder where Ancientone's body is? Why isn't it stuck behind this bridge?" He looked at his companions; their suddenly somber faces offered no answer. Realizing his questions had destroyed their mood of excitement, he grabbed an arm of each and squeezed, rasping out his words between almost-clenched teeth. "We've done it, my fellow adventurers! We've made it to the outside world that Sage hoped would be here."

"Yeah," said Strongheart, "but look at all those funny-looking trees mixed in with the spruce. No cones on them, either. Junk trees, they must be."

"At least there are some spruce," said Captain. "And maybe we'll find thicker groves of them when we explore farther. Look at this cone! No orange disease!" They hurriedly picked several other cones from low branches of nearby spruce. All looked invitingly clean and free of blight.

"Things are looking good," said Strongheart, "but what about this path? It could be an animal track except for the bridge. What kind of animal would lay down logs to help it cross a stream?"

"I can't think of any creature other than ourselves that would want to do that," said Captain. "Hey, maybe we'll find other Mumwalds down here! Oh...probably not. There aren't any webbed footprints in the dust. Well, no matter. Let's get a move on."

"About time," grumbled Muscles. "You two could talk all day."

Strongheart gave Muscles a playful shove with both hands. "Cheer up, Fatso!" Captain tensed as he saw a momentary flash of anger on Muscles' face, but a grudging, wry grin immediately followed and the limp response, "Watch it," signaled that Strongheart had gotten away with a bit of horseplay no other Mumwald would dare have tried.

The stream ahead looked too shallow and rocky for swimming or floating. They felt uneasy about following the path. So Captain led the others along the bank. It was rough going. The trees grew right down to the water. Tangles of fallen logs and saplings formed barricades that had to be circumvented. Finally, the Mumwalds gave up on land travel and entered the water again, this time to wade, not a simple task with webbed feet, but far easier than fighting the forest.

From time to time they stopped to inspect cones, not finding any that were blighted. Soon they reached a point where they could look down their waterway and see a lake. Before the stream poured into the lake, another log bridge crossed. They stopped before they reached the bridge. They could see just well enough through the trees to understand why a lake had formed here. A huge barren scar on the mountainside ahead and to the right indicated that a gigantic mudslide had oozed down into the valley and blocked the path of the stream sometime in the fairly distant past.

"A beautiful lake," whispered Strongheart. "A bit bigger than ours, I think."

"What are all those green things messing up the water close to the shore?" said Muscles.

"Those are lily pads," explained Captain. "When I was young, we had a few in our lake, but Sage had us clean them out for some reason."

They rested quietly for a few moments. Now that their splashing and talking had ceased, they became aware of odd noises—a combination of shouts and thuds and clunks and squeals—drifting through the trees from their right. "Let's sneak over that way," whispered Captain.

This time they had no choice but to struggle straight through the forest. They didn't want to go on up to the bridge and then follow the path that was presumably there, for Sage had warned them against being too bold. Nor did he want them to try to make contact with any creature until after they had reported their observations to him. He wanted to let their findings bounce around in his memory to see if they jarred anything loose. The scouts shoved and scrambled and burrowed through the trees until they came close to the edge of the wood, where they hid in a knot of fallen logs. Between them and the upward sloping mountainside was a large boulder field, barren of trees. Many of the rocks were far bigger than a Mumwald. It was from among them that the strange noises rose. As the explorers settled into their spying, they saw rocks and clods fly through the air from various spots in the field. Every now and then they caught glimpses of the creatures throwing the missiles.

"Weird things."

"Are they playing or fighting?"

"They're really ugly."

Presently, a thrower quit and came over to sit on a log by a path at the edge of the boulder field. The Mumwalds noticed then that others were there, seemingly observing the proceedings in the boulder field.

"I wonder why that one sat down," said Captain.

"Maybe he got hit. Do you suppose it's a game in which one has to...."

Muscles wasn't much interested in the action. "Yeah, yeah," he interrupted with a snarl, "but just look at them! They're so little and thin it would be fun to roll right into them and crush them."

Captain looked at Muscles disgustedly. If Captain had been like Stargazer, he would have started thinking about a possible connection between Muscles' attitude and the idea of sin. But instead, the leader simply turned his attention back to the creatures. The largest they had seen stood about a foot tall. They looked like two fur-covered sticks crossed over each other and slanted upward, like the letter X. Where the sticks crossed, there was a ball the size of a big orange. At each of the four ends of the sticks was a hand or foot; they all looked the same—four hands-feet. Each had long toes-fingers with sharp claws.

Their faces were on one side of the orange-sized balls where the two sticks crossed. And the strangest thing! Each had only one big eye, which looked like half a walnut bulging out of the ball. Somewhere among the shaggy reddish-brown fur must have been a mouth, nose, and ears, but they were hidden from view.

After several more of the creatures had left the rocks to sit and watch, the throwers hopped or flipped themselves on top of the boulders they had been hiding behind and began jumping up and down and squealing in hideous, high-pitched tones that made the Mumwalds cover their hearing mechanisms. The screeching revealed mouth openings in the creatures either under or over the eye, which seemed odd.

"I guess it was a game," said Strongheart.

Muscles scowled, "They must be awful stupid to play a game like that." Suddenly one of the creatures screamed something. They all took off running along a path to the north. It didn't matter which pair of hands-feet they ran on. They could be going along nicely, then suddenly do a flip and start racing along upside down, or so it seemed. This explained why the mouth was sometimes above and sometimes below the eye. Once in a while they even went along on all four hands-feet; then they appeared to be spiders that had lost half their legs. And they could bend over forward or backward to walk on all fours. Sometimes the eye would look down, sometimes up.

"Amazing!" said Strongheart. "I'd hate to get in a race with one of them"

"Yeah," said Muscles, "but a wrestling match would be all right."

Captain jerked to attention. "Look! The sun is close to dropping behind the mountain. Soon it will be sundown. We must get back."

10

Captain's Report

When the three explorers staggered panting out of the passage, they found the whole batch of Mumwalds waiting. Cheers and claps sounded. Motherone and Stargazer stood back from the crowd, unsure of how to react. Muscles saw Motherfour, went over, and took her hand in his. A slight, proud smile slipped onto his face.

"You're a bit late," said Sage, when the crowd had quieted.

"Yes, but what news we bring!" answered Captain with unusual gusto.

"Tell us all!"

As soon as everyone had found a sitting spot, Captain described what they had seen. After he had finished, Sage said, "A very interesting report. You three are to be praised for a job done well." He paused for a moment, staring thoughtfully at the cliff. "Now, the first thing we must do, if we're to talk about this other valley, is name the unknowns there—well, one isn't actually an unknown. You mentioned a strange kind of tree that had no cones. That is, I suspect, an aspen. I've not bothered to teach you its name because it is the type of tree we do not allow to grow in our valley. You know you have been ordered to pull out the little seedlings with the heart-shaped leaves. These would grow into aspen. They are useless to us. Now, let's see. We need a name for the creatures you saw. They don't jog any memory in me, so we'll invent a new one. How about 'Torwinks'? Yes—Torwinks it will be. Any questions?"

No Mumwald spoke.

"All right. What we must do now is set our attention on the purpose for your trip. You have given us ample reason to believe that this new valley contains a rich supply of untainted cones, which would certainly solve our food problem and should also allay any concerns about why we have had a few problems of late." As he said this, he looked back at Mother-one and Stargazer with what he thought was an innocent smile. Stargazer, however, read the expression as a smirk and, after Sage looked away, turned to whisper in his companion's ear. "Why does he keep trying to quiet our questions without really answering them?"

She whispered back, "I don't think he has any feeling whatsoever for 'why' questions."

Sage kept talking. "Now, the Torwinks seem to be intelligent creatures, from the little observation you conducted. I am just now wondering...." A puzzled look came over him. "My mind keeps asking a question, but I have no experience or wisdom from the past to help me answer it."

The assemblage was stone quiet. The Mumwalds had never seen Sage so genuinely perplexed, never heard Sage admit so openly a lack of wisdom about anything. Sage continued, this time as if talking to himself. "The question is, must we get permission from the Torwinks to gather cones from the valley they live in?"

Sneaky blurted, "We could sneak down and snatch some cones without asking."

"Yup, we sure could. Sounds good. Yup!" said Dumbell. "I could even sing while you others picked up cones. Be glad to. Yup!"

Captain said, "Whether or not they would care might depend on what they eat. We didn't see them munching on any cones."

"Or anything else, for that matter," said Strongheart.

"Yeah, but they sure didn't look like they could fight against us worth a hoot," said Muscles. "So I don't see...."

"Yes, yes," interrupted Sage. "We could go about this in many different ways. Your comments have helped me see the proper course. We have cultivated our little society for generation upon generation in order to live in harmony and without sin. We are about to enter an utterly new experience that will probably involve relationships that are not carefully defined by the principles nurtured in us. I insist that we go about this in the right way, which means we will attempt to bring this new experience within the circle of harmony that we already have."

Stargazer nudged Motherone and whispered, "Well, at least I'm impressed with this approach. He's actually doing some creative thinking." Motherone nodded.

Sage looked back at Stargazer and said, "My son, did you have a suggestion for us?"

"Uh, no, Sage, I was just saying to Motherone that I liked how you were going about this." He felt a rush of relief that Sage had caught him whispering this time rather than the time before. "It looks to me as if we just about have to approach the Torwinks and ask their permission."

"What if they can't talk?"

"Or what if they can talk but not in a way we can understand?"

"What if we can talk to them and we understand each other, but they refuse to let us gather cones?"

"What if—"

"Ho, my children," said Sage, waving his stubby old arms in front of his forehead. "Now you begin to see what new problems we face. We have never had to ask anything of anybody outside our own group except the Wondrous Star.

We live peaceably with the chipmunks and mice and trout. But we cannot talk to them so we and they ask nothing of each other. We must figure out how to get cones without causing any suffering for the Torwinks or being made to suffer ourselves."

Sneaky spoke up again. "Let's send a delegation of mothers. They'd be a lot more likely to wow those Torwinks than a bunch of us males. Isn't that right, good mother?" And he reached over to Motherfive sitting next to him, pinching her on the back.

"Sneaky, quit!" she snapped.

Other suggestions followed. Sage listened to all with respect. He smiled when Healer said they should take their cue from the chipmunks, who come up politely to the Mumwalds, sit erect on their haunches with forelegs bent, and supplicate for tiny morsels. So those little rascals do have a way to ask us for something, he thought. Muscles, however, spoiled the mood by returning to his refrain about how weak and vulnerable the Torwinks seemed in comparison to the robust Mumwalds. "When the eagle wants something from us, it swoops in and tries to take it without any 'if you please,'" he reminded them.

After discussion died down, Sage thanked them all for their help and called for a gathering the next day when the valley was half full of sun. He promised a decision on a plan of action by then. Dusk was rapidly turning to darkness as the crowd began to scatter. Sage called to Stargazer and asked him to accompany him back to the caves. They strolled slowly beside the calm waters of the lake. A trout after a water bug surfaced with a light splash.

"I appreciated your support in the meeting," said Sage. "It is important that we stand together now in these unusual times."

"It will be easy to support you if you stay on the path it appears you are on," said Stargazer. They walked on a few paces in silence. "But Sage, two things still bother me about what is going on."

"My, my. I suppose I know what one of them is. I keep hoping we've finished with those infernal questions about causes of things we cannot explain."

"You're right about the one. But the other one has to do with Muscles—and the idea of sin. Have you noticed how Muscles seems to be dwelling on one and only one theme in just about everything he says? He—" Suddenly Stargazer became aware of a Mumwald couple standing in the near darkness beside a large stone at the lake's edge. He couldn't tell who the two were, but he kept quiet until he and Sage were well past them. He lowered his voice when he continued. "Muscles' urge to fight others is very troubling. He really wants to hurt someone. Isn't he perilously close to sin?"

"It is interesting that you have picked up on that," said Sage, glad to be back in the role of mentor. "I have not discussed this aspect of our condition with anyone, but it would have come up in your training in time. You see, when we say we have developed a state of sinlessness, we mean we are able to live without causing any serious suffering within our society. We recognize, however, that discordant ideas and imaginings flitter through many Mumwalds' minds at times. If the thoughts or fantasies were allowed to be expressed in action, our harmonious lives would be disrupted. So far, our nurturing processes have succeeded well in channeling only positive mind productions into actions and in suppressing negative impulses altogether. The events of the last day or two have evidently jarred Muscles deeply enough that he is expressing many suppressed thoughts and feelings. It would be most enlightening to be able to find out what he has been dreaming lately, but it is doubtful that even I could get him to tell me—if he remembers his dreams at all. Yes, you are quite right. He is dangerously close to slipping into sin. He must be watched closely."

"Our forefathers in the Land Beyond must be rather nervous, watching us, waiting to see if we regress."

"Yes, and Great Maker is surely keeping his spiritual fingers crossed. However, I am confident that we can meet this situation with sufficient energy and innovation that we will come out well. I did want to ask you...well, I mean...uh, have you become aware of any others whom we should be especially watchful of?"

Stargazer thought he knew very well who Sage was wondering about, but he wasn't ready to say that rebellious thoughts had boiled to the top in Motherone. Even steady, old Sage might overreact if he knew what she had been saying. "Oh, no, not exactly," he said evasively, "but I am worried about how the questions Motherone and I have raised have upset a number of us. You said a moment ago that we have succeeded in keeping negative impulses from leading us into actions that would cause suffering. It seems, though, that words themselves are a form of action that have caused us some grief lately."

Sage stopped. The path had left the lakeshore and entered the forest between the lake and the caves. The faint light of the myriad stars no longer aided them. They had been walking by habit rather than by sight. "Hmmm," said Sage, putting out a hand to halt his colleague. "I hadn't thought about that. Speaking isn't the full-blown type of action I was talking about, but it certainly is closer to that kind of action than purely private thoughts."

"Yes, it's as if words were a bridge into the future, leading us into certain types of action if we care to take that bridge. They are a bridge between what is possible and what becomes actual."

"Aha. Brilliant! And there are several bridges we can choose from right now, depending on which possibilities we want to try to bring into the actual events of the future."

"And, you know, it is odd that all this is linked to the past too. The past limits the possibilities for the immediate future."

"My, my. You are getting in deep. But go ahead."

"Well, a spruce seed can't produce a chipmunk, but it can evidently help produce a spruce tree that is not an exact duplicate of former spruce trees. You and I can sit here and dream up new things for Mumwalds to do in the future, but what we inherit from the past cramps our style. We aren't suddenly going to get these chunky bodies to fly like the eagle or to swim continuously underwater like the trout. But we could come up with rules for a new game, for instance. We can bring some newness into our lives, but only so much. As we try to figure out which possibilities can really be brought into actuality in the near future, we must take a close look at the past."

"Yes, yes. As we walk across that bridge into the future, we are...we are...."

"Walking backwards into the future? Is that what you're trying to say?"

"I think so. Hmmm. This way of looking at things will help me in my decision making. Thank you, Stargazer. You have once again—"

"Uh, Sage, we've kind of gotten—uh, we'd better get moving again. Here, let me have your arm. Now, uh...you see, I was trying to get at whether or not the hurt that comes from the use of words is the result of sin. Do you see what I'm driving at?"

"Why, yes, I think I do. Yes, I think I do."

"Yup. I think I do too," blurted a voice out of the darkness immediately ahead of them. "Yup, I've been listening to you fellers. You sure know how to twirl words around in your heads. I don't reckon—"

"Excuse us, Dumbell," said Sage, groping with one hand outstretched to try to touch Dumbell. "Are you just standing there, or were you walking very slowly back to your cave?"

"Gosh, just standing, my good man. The smell of the spruce in the dark gets these little goose bumps going all over my sphere. Gets me all revved up for a good night's sleep. So if you gentlemen would please just step on by and leave me to my goose bumps, I'd appreciate it. Yup, I would."

"Thank you," said Sage, trying to feel apologetic. His groping hand had found Dumbell, and he now led Stargazer around the spruce lover. As they looked ahead along the path, they could see the dimly lit cliff wall above a black cave mouth. "So," said Sage. "Where were we? Oh, I was saying that I understood what you were saying. Hmmm. Bless me, I think I do understand, but I certainly don't like it. You're suggesting that you and I and perhaps a couple of others have spoken words that caused others to suffer emotionally—and if we've done that, we've...we've...good Great Maker, that's unthinkable! I'm a sage and you're a sage-in-training! We're the last ones who should revert to a state of...we've been chosen precisely because everyone thought we would be the least likely to...."

"Sage, you've got to go ahead and say it. You're suggesting that we have sinned, aren't you? It snuck right in and got us without our realizing it."

"Oh, my son, my son. What are you saying? What have we done? Here, help me up into my cave. There we go. Thatta boy. That's good, that's good. Now leave me to a good night's sleep."

"But I'm not so sure, actually, that every use of words that causes emotional distress involves sin. Maybe it depends—"

"Enough! Git! Go to bed. We've much to do tomorrow."

11

The Way of the Chipmunk

The next day, as the shadow of the eastern cliff slowly approached the middle of the valley, Stargazer and Motherone left the cave area and plodded along the forest path on their way to the gathering in the theater. Stargazer was explaining Sage's reaction to the suggestion that a few of the Mumwalds, including Sage himself, had actually sinned. "It amazed me, Motherone. Sage was being so rational, so lucid in his explanations, and I thought he was being very open to some new thoughts. But this one threw him for a total loop. He couldn't even say the word *sin* when it needed to be used in a personal confession. In fact, after a few moments of confusion, his repression mechanism seemed to snap into action. I started to try to refine the insight, but he dismissed me abruptly, and he seemed almost giddy!"

"My worst fears about him are being confirmed," said Motherone. "He will never be able to lead us through this mess. Why, he'll—"

"Hold it! I don't want to hear what I think you're about to say. Let's see what frame of mind he's in this morning at the meeting. Maybe he was just overtired last night. It was a long, pressure-packed day. We aren't in a very good position to understand the burden that decision making puts on our leader."

All Motherone said in reply was, "Pshaw. You'll see."

As soon as all the Mumwalds had settled on the rock ledges, Sage wasted no time in getting down to business. "I have carefully thought about what we discussed yesterday, my children. We have a choice between two basic paths. One is the way we relate to the chipmunks, mice, trout, and all the birds but the eagle: we will call this the Way of the Chipmunk. It is a way of peace, of harmony—above all, of live and let live. Second is the way we relate to the eagle. The Way of the Eagle is a way of fear and fighting, of wanting what another has and trying to take it by force."

"Fine thinking, my good man, fine thinking. Yup, I probably couldn't have done as well myself, although—"

"Dumbell, thank you for the compliment, but now please let me finish." The addle-brained one squeezed his lips together in a self-satisfied smile. Sage continued. "In accord with our state of sinlessness, we, of course, must choose the Way of the Chipmunk. Great Maker would have us try this way, and there is little doubt that this will lead to success if we follow it prudently. Once again, I will appoint three of you to go to the valley of the Torwinks, this time on a peace mission. Captain, you will lead, of course. Strongheart, you will go, too, partly because you are so fearless and partly because you observe well. Muscles, I'm asking you to stay here this time, for we may need your great strength later."

Sage's flattery of Muscles was mostly a ruse. Actually, he knew that Muscles' grumpy and often hostile nature would be entirely inappropriate for this new mission. He might say or do something that would needlessly upset the Torwinks.

"In place of Muscles, I want Motherfive to go. She is soft of tongue, young, and strong. Perhaps a female will help warm the hearts of the Torwinks in ways that the males can't, as Sneaky suggested yesterday. Are there any questions up to this point?"

"If our languages are different, how are we to talk to them?" asked Captain.

"Truly, Captain, I'm not sure. That's one of the greatest stumbling blocks to the Way of the Chipmunk. I've spent most of the night pondering the problem and do have several suggestions, however. Use motions of your hands and other parts of your body. Try to express things with your face. Draw pictures in the air or in the dust. Or, who knows? Perhaps you can quickly teach the Torwinks some of our language, or they can teach you some of theirs. We have no experience to tell us how difficult that might be, but we do know that our own young pick up our language very quickly."

That seemed to satisfy Captain. Final arrangements were made. Sage gave the adventurers much more time for this mission. If they weren't back by the middle of the fourth day, he would send a group down to find out why. By straight-up sun time, the Mumwalds had collected around the passage entrance once again, but they were not in such a gay mood this time as they bid farewell to their delegation. This mission didn't seem quite so full of hope as the last one. The thrill of adventure had given way to a sense of foreboding, despite Sage's upbeat attitude. They knew what to expect from the lesser animals—but other talking, intelligent creatures? They weren't so sure about them.

As Captain led Strongheart and Motherfive into the passage, Mothertwo looked around and muttered to herself, "Oh dear, now where has Mischief gotten off to?"

Inside the passage the three stopped for a moment to get used to the dark. Captain casually asked, "You do have the basket of cones, don't you, Strongheart?" Though they knew cones were available in the forest below, they were taking a small supply of their own as a precaution against unforeseen problems.

"Yes." Strongheart was carrying the basket with his right hand. He put his left hand into the basket to make sure none of the cones were about ready to fall out. "Yeow!" he hollered.

Motherfive, in the middle, jumped forward against Captain. "Wh-what happened?" sputtered the leader.

"Something bit me when I put my hand in the basket." With that, Strongheart held the basket high, spun around, and rushed out into the light. Mumwalds crowded around him. They saw nothing in the basket except cones. Then Sneaky reached over and carefully lifted out two of the cones. There, holding his fat little fingers over his eyes, was a tiny ball of white fur.

"Mischief! You come out of there!" cried Mothertwo. "You will be the death of me yet!" And once again, she held him upside down until his top—even the fur—was very pink and very painful.

The peace party set out again, first to the dead-end wall of the passage, then up onto the shelf, and finally down the long descent to the falls. Captain and Strongheart kept talking to Motherfive as long as the noise of the falls let them. They thought this would help keep her from being afraid. The only time she was afraid, though, was when she had to jump into the water and swim through the falls. Captain showed her the way, and Strongheart, the basket handle held in his mouth, stayed right beside her. She had no trouble.

When they approached the first log bridge, Captain swam toward the bank on his right. The others followed. They scrambled up to the path and stepped brisky across the bridge. The plan was to move boldly right up to the Torwinks, wherever they were. Since it had appeared that the Torwinks played on the side of the valley west of the stream, Sage and Captain had decided that they might live on the east side. Captain was hoping now that the path through the mixed aspen and spruce would lead them right to a batch of nests or caves or whatever shelter the Torwinks used. The Mumwalds certainly didn't want to be caught sneaking around through the trees or down the stream, for that would make the Torwinks suspicious.

The path at first headed straight east through the trees, but before it hit the abrupt, steep rise of the eastern mountainside, it turned toward the south. The Mumwalds could see a long way down the path in this new direction. No evidence appeared to indicate where the Torwink homes might be. In fact, though the path was clearly well-used, the scratchy markings in the dust seemed to be at least a day or two old. "Perhaps we didn't guess right," mumbled Captain as he waddled quickly along.

Suddenly, a rustling sound came from high up in a thicket of aspen in the direction of the stream. The three scouts stopped instantly and peered into the shadowy treetops, moving their spheres back and forth to see past trunks and branches and leaves. The rustling continued for several seconds and then quit as quickly as it had begun. The Mumwalds shifted to and fro along the path, trying to get a better view, but none of them spotted anything unusual. Finally, Strongheart held his arms and hands in a shrugging gesture, and the three proceeded down the path, a bit more slowly this time, with sight and hearing tuned more to the forest. They soon came to a point where the blue lake water sparkled through the trees ahead, and the path turned to the west. As they followed the curve and approached the second log bridge, they thought they heard more rustling sounds, faint this time, from upstream. They didn't bother to stop but instead flapped their way across the bridge.

12

An Unfriendly Reception

A few strides past the bridge they burst out from under the protective covering of the trees and into the open by the boulder field where they had seen the Torwinks the day before. This time none of the odd X-figures were in sight. Only an eerie silence met them. Captain stopped first and his companions came up to stand beside him. No bluebird sailed within sight. Nor did even one chipmunk pop its head from behind a rock to inspect them. They looked at each other with eyes wide with wondering and a hint of apprehension. Side by side they took a few cautious steps along the path beside the boulder field, swinging their spheres from left to right and back to keep an eye on both trees and boulders.

Suddenly a Torwink hopped out from behind a boulder a short stone's throw in front of them and then hopped back into hiding just as fast. Another vaulted to the top of a boulder directly to their right and immediately disappeared. A shrill whistle pierced the air. The Mumwalds stood motionless as Torwinks then appeared from all directions. Some swung down from high in trees, others raced out from the boulders, and many flip-flopped out from behind tree trunks. Two dozen of the stick figures rushed up to form a tight circle around their fat visitors, who were trying their best to put natural-looking smiles on their faces and keep them there. The three stood with their backs to each other, forming something of a triangle. They towered six inches above the tallest Torwink. No expressions were visible through the thick, shaggy fur on the latters' faces.

To show that he was leader, Captain pointed to himself and said, "Captain. Captain." He turned and pointed to himself and his two comrades with a circular motion. "Mumwalds. Mumwalds."

None of the Torwinks made a move or a sound. Each with his single, unblinking eye silently stared at the encircled newcomers. Finally, Captain, his mouth now dry and his voice almost cracking, managed to say, "We come as friends." He held out both his hands with palms up, hoping a Torwink would come forward and lay two claw-hands palms down in his in the usual Mumwald greeting. No Torwink came forward, however. They all continued to stand and stare in what the Mumwalds began to feel was an ominous manner.

Now that they were close, the Mumwalds noticed that some of the Torwinks had darker brown fur than others, and these were usually smaller than the ones with reddish-brown fur. Several of the dark brown ones carried tiny, young Torwinks, who rode right on top of the orange-sized ball of the mother.

Without warning, one of the Torwinks started squealing. The others joined in, even the young. As they squealed, some doubled over, others put two hands-feet in front of their mouths. A few turned flips on the outer edge of the crowd.

Strongheart gritted his teeth, still trying to hold his lips in a smile. "I think they're laughing at us," he said softly.

"Yes," said Captain. "Perhaps we should try to laugh with them." The Mumwalds forced themselves to croak as naturally as they could. This only made the Torwinks wilder in their laughter. The Mumwalds became silent, feeling very uncomfortable.

Finally, the Torwinks settled down and re-formed their tight circle. Captain decided to try again, this time with a rather grim look on his face. He pointed to himself and held up one finger. Then he pointed around the circle at various Torwinks. "Who is your leader?" he asked. He touched his mouth and then turned his finger toward the Torwinks. "I want to talk to your leader."

Still, no one responded. More awkward seconds passed. One Torwink uttered a quick string of sounds in a squeaky voice. Captain glanced at his two companions and saw that they hadn't understood any words either. Other Torwinks began chattering and waving their upper arms-legs excitedly.

"I think they have an idea to do something," said Mother-five warily.

Several Torwinks came up to each Mumwald, some grabbing hold of arms and pulling them out of their triangle, others then getting behind the spheres. They half shoved and half dragged the three along the path toward the south end of the boulder field, being neither exactly rough nor exactly gentle.

Despite their height and tremendous bulk advantage, none of the Mumwalds resisted. After all, theirs was a peace mission, and they weren't being harmed. Captain's hope was that they were finally being taken to the Torwink leader. When they came to the turn in the path that led to the second log bridge the Mumwalds had crossed earlier, the Torwinks veered off with their guests—or captives—to the right, into the huge stones. Each Mumwald was placed facing north on the south side of a different boulder. Behind them, only a few paces across a stand of marshy grass, was the lake.

Five of the largest reddish-brown creatures separated from the group. They pointed to themselves and then to the Mumwalds and made overhand sweeping motions with their upper appendages, all the while chattering and squealing unintelligible noises.

Strongheart was the first to catch on. "I have the feeling they want to play that rock throwing game with us."

"How frightful!" said Motherfive.

When they finished their gyrations, the five Torwinks trotted to positions behind boulders some distance to the north. The remainder of the crowd went to the edge of the field to watch. A piercing whistle sounded again. Immediately, stones and clods shot toward the Mumwalds.

"We'd best play along as well as we can," said Captain. He picked up a rock and slung it side arm. It flew off to the side toward the spectators but fell far short. Squeals of laughter erupted from the crowd. Strongheart and Motherfive began throwing, too, but neither was effective. They were not used to throwing. Except for their mud fights, the only time they ever threw something at a target was when an eagle attacked, and that was too rare to keep them in practice.

The Torwinks, of course, were experts. They knew that direct, horizontal tosses were useless so long as the Mumwalds stayed behind their boulders, but they also knew that the spherical bodies still made excellent targets for lobs.

Soon, a soft clod arced down on Strongheart and shattered on his top above his right eye. He immediately started to walk over to the edge of the field, as he thought Torwinks had done the day before when they got hit. The spectators gestured agitatedly and several from the crowd hurried to him and pushed him back toward his boulder.

"Well, I guessed wrong about that rule," Strongheart said, gingerly touching the sore spot above his eye. "What do I do now?"

"Keep throwing!" shouted Captain worriedly, his sphere tilted upward watching for well aimed missiles. "They're moving closer now that they know we aren't very good throwers."

Strongheart shook his head and heaved a rock in the general direction of the attackers. Captain hopped quickly out into the open to the left of his boulder to survey the field again, and before any of the enemy could take direct aim, he spun back to relative safety. He had seen two of the Torwinks slowly moving up straight in front of the Mumwalds. Two others were easing around to the west near the rising mountainside, and the fifth was dancing from boulder to boulder toward the forest side. None of them were being careful to stay protected.

Captain looked at Motherfive. "They're trying to—"

"Owww! Ohhh!" cried the good mother. Two rocks hit her at once, one very close to her top. She plopped down on her bottom in a daze.

"I'm not so sure this is just a game," said Strongheart.

Each advancing Torwink was now slinging stones with two hands-feet at once, and one dexterous fellow stood on one hand-foot and lobbed simultaneous clods with his three free hands-feet. Soon the Torwinks would be firing at them from three directions. Captain saw only one alternative to getting pummeled. "Quickly!" he yelled. "To the lake before they get to our sides. Maybe we can outswim them!" He started to scramble backwards.

"I'm...not sure...I can make it," said Motherfive, gasping. Captain hurried to her and helped her to her feet. He started pulling her by the hand. A barrage of dirt and rocks shot straight at them as they moved into the open.

Strongheart shouted, "You two get to the lake! I'll try to slow them down and then follow!"

When the Torwinks realized what was happening, they squealed angrily. The five fighters raced along paths between boulders toward the retreating Mumwalds, throwing as they ran. Strongheart crouched as low as he could behind the last large boulder. A small bush of sage brush at the side of the boulder helped hide him. Peeking cautiously through the sage, he could see that two of the Torwinks were dashing almost uncontrollably down a path that led right past him. He crouched down, propped one webbed foot against the boulder and leaned forward on the knuckles of both hands. At just the right moment he thrust forward with all his strength. Immediately, he curled up into a ball as he had seen Roller do. One Torwink was close behind the other. The big Mumwald caught them both with the full ramming force of his roll. The light stick figures sailed off their feet and smacked hard into the next boulder.

The impact of the hit stopped Strongheart's roll. He pushed to his feet and headed at a fast wobble toward the lake. The other three Torwinks dashed from out of the boulder field. When they caught a glimpse of their two comrades lying motionless next to the boulder, they braked instantly. That was all the delay Strongheart needed to flop into the water. He paddled furiously through the lily pads that lined the shore, catching up with Captain and Motherfive just as they all reached open water.

When they finally looked back, they saw the Torwinks in disarray. The spectators were rapidly joining the three healthy fighters in the grass, some jumping wildly up and down, others searching frantically for objects to throw. Two or three females were ministering to the two fallen ones. High-pitched

screams and angry chattering filled the air. Finally, several males retreated to the boulder field and began gathering stones and clods, but by the time they returned to the lakeshore and started throwing, the swift paddlers were far out of range.

Not one Torwink entered the water to swim after them. In fact, they saw one Torwink put all his strength into a throw, slip, and get a hand-foot wet. He jumped up and screeched, flailing his wet limb about as if it had touched a hot rock.

"Ahhh," sighed Captain. "I believe we're safe for the moment."

Motherfive groaned. She had used up her last bit of energy. Strongheart moved in behind her to push her along with his powerful strokes. They floated now at a leisurely pace more toward the middle of the lake.

Strongheart raised the inevitable question. "How will we get back to our valley? They'll see us if we try to get ashore anywhere."

"And we lost our basket of food when they shoved us into the boulder field," whispered Motherfive.

"We can't last four days without getting awfully weak."

"Yes, I know," said Captain. "We can only wait until dark and hope we can sneak ashore then."

The Torwinks spread out along the shore. Some crossed the bridge to guard the shore on the other side of the stream. Several climbed trees for a better view. Two or three went into the forest and returned with long sticks. With these they reached into the lake and pulled lily pads to the shore. After letting most of the water drip off the pads, they started munching on them.

Nightfall came. The Mumwalds quietly floated close together in the middle of the lake, glad at least that a thunderstorm hadn't caught them out there. They could no longer see the Torwinks, but they could tell from noises that some, at least, were still spread out along the shore. A sliver of moon rose over the mountains to the east.

13

Escape

"It doesn't look good," said Captain. "I'm afraid our white fur makes us shine like little moons out here. I'm sure the Torwinks have no trouble seeing us, even though we can't see them."

"I've been thinking the same thing," said Strongheart. "But look at Motherfive. See how her gray fur blends in with the water? I doubt if she can be seen from very far."

"Then I must be the one to try to go for help," volunteered the brave mother. She had recovered much of her strength.

Thousands of stars glittered in the sky as the Mumwalds quietly formulated a plan. When they had finished, Captain and Strongheart began paddling slowly back toward the boulder field. Motherfive cut rapidly away from them, angling toward a point some distance to the east of where the stream entered the lake.

As the two male Mumwalds came close to being within throwing range of the Torwinks, a plunk sounded nearby. Drops of spray sprinkled them. "Good," whispered Strongheart. "But why didn't they wait until we are closer so they could do some damage?"

"Maybe they don't want to risk letting us get to shore and fighting them in the dark. You probably scared them to death the way you smashed into those two throwers."

"Humph. I doubt it. Their throwing arms still give them a tremendous advantage. Still, I suppose they might want to keep us out here until we get weak from hunger."

"True. And they may realize that their main supply of missiles is in the boulder field. If we'd meet them elsewhere, we'd have...."

"I see what you're getting at. But I'd like to think they aren't smart enough to figure all these things out. Hey, I haven't heard any splashes from Motherfive's direction, have you?"

"No, but it's a long way over there."

The air was stirring with a light breeze from the south, rippling the surface of the lake. The wind and the wave action gently moved Strongheart and Captain toward the hostile shore. They began treading lightly with their big, webbed feet so that they floated ever so slowly back against the wind toward the center of the lake.

* * *

By this time Motherfive had paddled her way close to the northeastern shore. She could see no movement on the shore. The only sounds were the soft lapping of the waves against the mud bank and the rustle of aspen leaves. She remained a few feet off shore for several minutes, listening and watching. Several large spruce trees shot up right at the edge of the bank, their roots nearest the water exposed by the erosion of the mud. She paddled quietly in a few feet closer, under the shadow of the trees, and stopped again.

From farther down the shore came the faint noises of chattering and splashing and swishing as the Torwinks tossed rocks and reached with sticks for lily pads. There was still no evidence that any of the stick creatures had taken up positions as far from the bridge as she was. She let the wind push her the rest of the way to the shore. As soon as her feet touched the mushy lake bottom, she carefully lifted her body out of the water. She was glad for the breeze. The gentle smacking of the waves helped cover the sound of the drips from her fur. With her right hand she grabbed hold of a tree root and with her left she grasped a clump of long, heavy-bladed water grass. One quick jerk of both wrists was all she needed to roll herself face down onto the grassy turf. She lay still for more seconds but heard nothing unusual.

Boosting herself to her feet, she squinted at the forest. Her plan was to walk through the forest more or less parallel to the path the three Mumwalds had plodded down earlier. The path itself would be too risky to use. As she peered into the trees, she began immediately to have doubts about that plan. Though it was terribly dark ahead of her, she could see enough to tell her that a tangled mess of low-lying branches and fallen limbs and tree trunks awaited her. Climber might be able to get through that and have fun doing it, but Mother-five knew she would never make it. Yet, she didn't dare follow the uncluttered bank to the path by the bridge.

She looked to her right. She had come ashore near where the steep mountainside met the valley floor. A small opening in the trees in that direction looked inviting. She entered it, feeling almost as closed in as she had in the tunnel that brought her into this valley. A half-dozen cautious steps brought her suddenly to a narrow opening in the trees. A rock ledge gleamed in the faint light. It was only a six-inch step up onto it at this point. She rolled herself up and looked to the north. The ledge sloped upward, getting higher above the valley floor and forming more of a cliff, but it kept going in the right direction for as far as she could see. She couldn't have built herself a better pathway, well lighted by the tiny moon and not seriously obstructed by fallen parts of trees. She uttered a little croak of delight as she waddled forth, not even being too careful about the noise she was making. Occasionally, she came to a spot where a deep, wide crack in the rock forced her to detour briefly into the forest that sloped upward above the cliff top.

Mumwalds were not made for broad jumping over cracks that wide. As she got close to the falls, she saw that the mountainside on her right, which had gradually become steeper and less thickly forested, had finally turned into a solid rock cliff looming above her. Only one thing concerned her. The incline of her ledge had led her up and up. She wondered if she wouldn't be too high above the stream when she got to the falls, if the pathway went that far.

She was right. The ledge did continue clear to the falls. When she got to the end, she could reach a stubby arm out and feel the cold water splatter on her hand. She looked down and then up. The path had brought her to a point almost halfway up the falls. She was nearly a hundred feet above the tunnel at the bottom of the falling water. She quickly stumbled back away from the edge and plopped onto her bottom, her back against the cliff rising above her. The pathway that had seemed such a blessing a short time before had led her into a seemingly impossible predicament.

* * *

Captain and Strongheart had meanwhile pushed themselves back to the center of the lake, where they came to rest—except they couldn't completely rest, for they had to continue a lazy paddling motion to keep from being blown to shore.

Strongheart broke the long silence they had maintained. "What do you make of all this?"

"Hmm?" said Captain, as if he'd been napping.

"What's going on here? I mean, how do you explain what's happening to us?"

Captain was fully awake now, but he was hardly up to answering such a question. Neither he nor his companion were among the more contemplative Mumwald spirits. He hadn't even thought to ask a "why" or "what's going on" question and he was surprised that Strongheart had come up with one. Finally, Captain said, "Let's leave that to Sage— and maybe Stargazer. They'll love to tackle your question."

"Stargazer maybe, but not Sage. Maybe I shouldn't say it, but the old fellow seems a bit befuddled by our new situation."

"Come, come, my friend. You mustn't talk against our revered leader. He'll find the right way for us to go, don't you worry."

Strongheart stared above the trees. He could see the top part of the falls sparkling in the moonlight. The sparkle did not reflect the way his own heart felt. "Uh, sorry, Captain. I didn't mean to sound uncertain about him. Still...."

"Let's just drop it and rest," said Captain quietly but firmly.

* * *

Trying to decide what to do, Motherfive sat for several minutes on the wide ledge with her back against the cliff towering above her. As she had waddled up the pathway, she had peeked over the edge periodically and she knew that batches of tall spruce sometimes grew on the valley floor below very close to the cliff. She thought about how Climber had let herself fall through the spruce branches that day the eagle had almost clamped its talons on her. The branches had broken her fall until she fell amongst the Mumwalds. But that would hardly work here. Motherfive would fall probably forty or fifty feet before she even began hitting spruce branches of any size, and by then her heavy body would have worked up such momentum that she would either break off smaller branches without a pause and be flattened against the ground or squashed against a big branch that refused to give way.

At the edge of their own lake, Mumwalds liked to jump off a certain large boulder they could climb up on. But that was only four or five feet above the water, and she grimaced when she remembered how the slap of the water hurt her back when she jumped just from that height. No way was she going to jump into the stream below the falls from a hundred feet above.

Slowly she got up and started walking back down the ledge, her sphere tilted slightly forward in discouragement. She hadn't gone more than a hundred feet when she was stopped by one of the large cracks in the rock. The cliff on her left had already turned back into the steep, lightly forested slope. In her excitement at getting near the end of the trail earlier, she hadn't even been aware of detouring into the forest to get around this crack. She leaned over and peered down into the abyss. The tiny moon was high enough in the eastern sky to shed a bit of light far into the hole. Motherfive jerked straight up excitedly and quickly shuffled into the forest to the end of the crack, where she halted abruptly and looked down again. It was difficult to tell, but she thought she could see well over halfway to the bottom. At this point, the valley floor was probably only about eighty feet below. Dirt had blown into the slit and had formed a more or less smooth slide going down at a steep angle—a monstrously steep angle, to be sure, but far better than a sheer drop and perhaps better than walking clear back to the lake and risking travel on the dirt path in the valley.

She sat again, in order to think through the situation. She could see several potential problems in using the slide. First, being round, she would almost certainly have a strong tendency to roll down rather than slide, and that would be a disaster. Second, she couldn't see all the way down, and the gap might narrow to the extent that she would become irretrievably stuck, or jagged rocks might jut up out of the dirt to slice her. Third, if she did manage to stay on her back or bottom all the way down, she would probably rub all the fur off and some of her skin. Fourth, she might be going so fast when she hit bottom that the danger of injury was great. Strangely, none of these dangers, nor even the whole batch taken together, daunted her in the least. She knew this was her way down. She knew there was a way to make it work.

And there was. It was quite simple. She looked around at the sloping forest floor and immediately saw what she needed, a stout stick about two feet long. Hopping up, she grabbed the stick. She squatted at the top of the slide, her bottom resting half on the dirt and half on the heels of her webbed feet. She gripped the stick tightly, one hand at one end and the other near the middle.

The other end of the stick she aimed at a rough spot on the left wall of the crack about two feet below her. With a brave little "whee," she shoved off. The broad bottoms of her feet acted like a toboggan. Just as she began to feel her speed picking up too much, she jammed the end of the stick into the rough spot on the rock wall, jolting herself to a stop. A

short distance ahead, she spotted another niche in the wall
that would catch her stick next. She again launched downward and halted her progress before she was out of control.
In this way she eased herself clear to the valley floor. The slide
remained wide enough and smooth enough all the way down.

"Wow! Wait till I tell the others about that trip!" she said to herself. And then she felt the ache in her arms from the strain of braking. "Ohhh," she moaned.

Quickly shaking off that moment of self-pity, she found that the tangle of fallen limbs, undergrowth, and live branches was not so thick right next to the cliff base. With little further difficulty, she reached the stream leading to the base of the waterfall and plopped in. The water felt cool and refreshing. Once through the falls, she reached onto the low ledge that led into the tunnel. The rock was wet and slippery. She couldn't find a good handhold to pull herself out of the water. With one hand paddling while the other felt along the slimy stone, she moved to her left. At last her fingers slipped into a crack in the rock. She grabbed hold with both hands, sighing deeply. Putting all her strength into the effort, she tugged and rolled herself up. She sat down against the rock wall. If only she had a cone to give her energy. But all she could do was rest a few minutes.

When she came out into the valley of the Mumwalds, she found Stargazer sitting by the passage entrance.

"Stargazer, I'm so glad to see you," she said, rather weakly.

"Motherfive!"

"Wh-what are you doing here?" she asked in a tired voice.

"Sage thought we should take turns keeping watch here." Stargazer peered into the passage. "Where are the others?"

"That's a long story. We must go to Sage quickly. Then I'll tell all."

They woke Sage in his cave. He saw to it that Motherfive ate before she told what had happened.

14

Rescue

everal times during Mother-five's story Sage shook his head gravely. After she had finished, he said, "What you say forms a great mystery in my mind. I don't understand why the Torwinks treated you the way they did."

"It's hard to say what their original intentions were," said Stargazer.

"If they had wanted to kill us, wouldn't they have ambushed us as soon as we got onto the path by the boulder field? And wouldn't all of them have been in on the attack?" asked Motherfive.

"Maybe, maybe not," said Stargazer. "They might have wanted at least a chance to get close to you and see if they could communicate with you. When they found they couldn't, they may have decided to have some fun with you."

"You mean, have some fun at our expense!"

"Perhaps they didn't know how threatening the game seemed to you three. Maybe they wouldn't let Strongheart sit down after he got hit because there is some other rule governing sit-downs. We just don't know why they acted the way they did."

Sage shook his head. "We mustn't waste more time wondering about that now. We must think of a way to get Captain and Strongheart out of there."

"Uh—I suppose that means you want me to go wake Muscles?" said Stargazer.

"Not yet," said the old leader. He turned to see that Motherfive had her eyes closed as she sat. He reached over and patted her gently on the arm. "Motherfive, you have done well. Go now to your cave and rest. Stargazer and I will think about what to do next."

Sage scooted to the entrance of his cave and looked up at the moon and stars. He went back over everything he had been told about the valley of the Torwinks. While Stargazer continued to brood about why the Torwinks had acted as they had, the aged leader did what he was best at: he formulated a plan of action to rescue the two lake-bound Mumwalds in the valley below. Finally, he spoke softly, "Go wake Muscles, Sneaky, Jester, Motherthree, and...yes, we must have Motherfive too. Bring them here."

Stargazer twisted his sphere so that he could look at his mentor. "Did...didn't you want...did you want to ask me...?"

"No, no. I need no help on this one. I have it all worked out. Please get the others."

Without further questioning, Stargazer left and soon brought the five to Sage's cave in the darkness. Sage told them what had happened and what he wanted them to do. It was an hour before first light when he said, "Go now, Muscles, and lead the others to the rescue. Do exactly as I have told you. Above all, don't fight unless you have to. We want all of you back safely."

Muscles frowned. He wasn't used to being a leader. "Yeah," he said. "Well...uh...come on...into the forest everyone," and he plodded out of the cave area and into the trees. The moon was far into the western sky by now, but still helped cast a pale light on the valley. Before long, each of the five members of the rescue squad had found a solid, thick stick about a foot long. They gathered at the edge of the trees.

Jester held his stick up high in front of Sage. "So this is what our forefathers used to call a 'club', eh?"

"That's right, my son. Now remember, you are to use that only for self-defense. We must maintain our state of sinlessness." He paused for a moment as he remembered his discussion with Stargazer, but immediately he shook off the memory and went on. "Do not hit anyone with those unless you absolutely have to in order to protect yourself or another Mumwald."

Muscles looked at the others with a face contorted by a sense of confusion and a touch of anger, but he didn't say anything. He just waved his stick in a "follow me" gesture, grunted, and started down the path toward the tunnel entrance. They stopped at the lakeshore long enough for the three males to spread mud all over each other to dull their gleaming white fur.

Muscles led the way into the passage, with Motherthree, then Motherfive behind him. Sneaky hustled in front of Jester in order to be fourth, right behind his favorite mother. His right hand was just reaching out to pinch her above her right arm when she whirled halfway around and hissed with friendly menace, "Cease and desist, you not-so-sneaky slime-sucker."

Sneaky thrust both arms straight up in the air in the narrow tunnel and whooped. "Whoa, O Merciful Wondrous Star! Save me from this vicious creature."

Jester laughed. "You'd be safer surrounded by ten Torwinks than you are following that one tough mother!"

From the front of the line they heard a huge, protracted growl, followed by, "That's enough, you clowns. This isn't a Mumwald mud fight we're heading into. Get your minds on our business!" Sneaky and Jester stood rigid in mock attention, the darkness covering their smirking faces. They said nothing more.

It was darker when they reached the falls. The moon had gone down behind the mountains to the west. Daybreak was still half an hour away. Muscles led the way again, showing the ones who hadn't been there how to paddle through the falls. They floated to the first bridge and climbed out of the water onto the west bank, gambling that no Torwinks were out and about in this part of the valley. Hearing nothing out of the ordinary, they crossed the bridge and set down their clubs. Silently, the males daubed more mud on the spots washed clean by the water. Then all five Mumwalds grabbed hold of one of the bridge logs and pulled it across the stream to their side. They did the same with the other three logs.

As they headed down the path toward the lake, tightly clutching their clubs, all but Muscles used their free hands to clutch the next Mumwald ahead. With a firm tenderness, Sneaky gripped Motherfive's wrist above her club-holding hand, giving it a series of quick, light squeezes. This time she didn't hiss at him or pull her hand away. Instead, he felt a slight shove in his direction. Their progress was slow because of the extreme darkness now. Eventually, though, they came without incident to the bend where the path turned west to reach the second bridge. They could now see the lake water shimmer through the trees in the starlight. Soon after they had padded softly around the bend, they stopped. All seemed peaceful ahead—no unusual sounds or motions. They cautiously edged ahead seventy-five feet or so before stopping again and taking stock. Everything still seemed clear. They were perhaps another seventy-five feet from the bridge, but it wasn't nearly that far straight through the trees to the lake. In the dim light, it appeared that a Mumwald could get through the forest easily at this point. Muscles turned to the two mothers and gave them a light shove in the direction of the lake. The three males stood still at the edge of the path and watched the silhouettes of the females wind their way toward the water. Soon the two gray-furred creatures slipped quietly into the lake and began paddling toward two small, white blobs bobbing far out ahead of them.

* * *

As soon as the rescue party had taken its leave, Stargazer left Sage, for the old one was exhausted. The younger Mumwald felt wide awake, and Sage hadn't ordered him to renew his vigil at the tunnel entrance, so he waddled softly down the line of cave openings to the next to last one. It was not his. Inching his way into the blackness, he kept one hand against the south wall of the cave and the other hand extended palm first in front of his nose. Shortly, a faint, sweet odor made his nose twitch. He smiled. The sound of heavy, regular breathing, interrupted now and then by a tiny snort, came from directly in front of him. Three more cautious steps and his fingers tingled as they touched fur. He drew back his hand and pressed his lips hard against a Mumwald top.

The sphere he had kissed jerked suddenly and rolled swiftly away from the cave wall. "Who...who is it?" came a frightened whisper from the mouth of Motherone. "Stargazer, that better be you!"

"It is, it is." He tried to reassure her with a grin she couldn't see.

She looked outside and could tell that the moon no longer shone on the cave entrance. "Climber could be waking up soon," she said. "This isn't any time for you and me to—"

"No, no, not that," he said, feeling his way to her and taking her by the arm. He led her to the cave entrance. "I need to talk." He sat facing her right ear directly and told her in low tones what had been going on.

When he ended, Motherone said immediately, "I can't believe that Sage didn't even talk his plans over with you before putting them into effect."

Though Stargazer had felt a twinge of chagrin when Sage had abruptly ordered him to get the five rescue squad members, he didn't let Motherone know that. He simply said, "Sage is excellent at making plans of action. You know he is. Let's not get off on that. I want to know what you think about these Torwinks. What's going on in their minds?"

"Well...they certainly sound like mean-spirited little creatures to me."

"Yes. That would make them full of sin, wouldn't it? If they meant to do us harm, there isn't anything tricky or subtle about it. Their society would be way behind ours. They wouldn't have learned to obliterate sin."

"That sounds right."

"But what if we just don't know how to interpret their actions? What if, in their minds, they were simply being hospitable, trying to include us in what they considered a fun experience?"

"That's awfully far-fetched."

"But at least possible, wouldn't you say?"

"Oh, yes, I suppose so. What are you driving at?"

"If sin isn't at the root of our problem with them, then what is? I'll answer that: it's our lack of ability to communicate with them. And that's a natural limitation we have no control over."

"OK. Yes, that sounds reasonable. But…."

"Don't you see how this ties in with our problem with the cones we eat? Maybe that too is a problem that we have no control over. Maybe it just happened. Not because of our sin, I mean, but just happened. The cone blight is part of nature's working. The blight itself is a natural phenomenon that has a right to exist. It wouldn't cause any special distress in most places."

"True—as far as animals are concerned. But I would say the trees are distressed."

"Hmm. Very good. I hadn't thought of that. The blight damages the tree cones and the cones damage us. The tree seems to be a higher form of life—more complex, I mean— than the blight, and we are a higher form of life than the tree. Does that mean the blight really doesn't have a right to exist, because it is damaging to higher forms of life?"

"I certainly don't know. It might depend on what is causing the blight to do what it does."

"Yes, yes. It depends on whether the blight is part of the supposed plan of nature that Great Maker devised in the beginning, or whether…oh, wow…whether it might in some way be an agent of No Place, if that is possible."

"That's scary. What does the received wisdom have to say about that?"

"Sage hasn't mentioned such a thing at all. Hey! Another thought just hopped into my mind. Maybe Great Maker doesn't really create everything. That would help explain why

He doesn't control all events in such a way that only good things happen to us. Maybe the world is just somehow here and Great Maker is part of it, just as we are. That's a real mind-stretcher, isn't it? Hmm. Do you think I ought to approach Sage with these ideas?"

"Ha, it would probably be of little use. It sounds as if you are leading up to saying that we shouldn't be calling our supreme being Great *Maker*." Thoughts of Healer's tradition surged into her head. She wanted to say something about it but didn't dare. "Even if Sage could follow your train of thought, I doubt if he'd be interested at all. You know how—"

At that moment, a tiny, sleepy, croaking voice from in the cave said, "Mommie, you waked me up."

Motherone pursed her lips together and reached over to clamp a hand over Stargazer's mouth. They waited silently. No more sounds came from within. Stargazer gently took Motherone's hand from his mouth, kissed it, and whispered very quietly, "I'll talk to you later." Then he left.

* * *

The moment Muscles saw the two mothers start swimming out to Strongheart and Captain, he tugged on Jester and Sneaky, pulling them toward the second bridge. With their camouflaged bodies, they reached the bridge without being discovered. Evidently, as they had hoped, all the Torwinks had gathered on the western side of the stream as the night wore on. Quickly, the Mumwalds dismantled the bridge. The rippling stream covered the noise of the scraping logs as they dragged them to their side. When they were done, they crept back to the point where the mothers had entered the forest. A faint gray light appeared. They had timed everything just right. Peering through the forest at the lake, they waited anxiously. After some time they realized that the white blobs were moving toward them. The mothers remained invisible.

Without warning, a shrill whistle sounded from across the bridge. Rustling noises and chattering squeaks carried down to the Mumwalds. Little splashes started dotting the lake water. The Torwinks' rocks were falling far short, but they continued peppering the water anyway. In the dim light, the Mumwalds could see two Torwinks dash to where the bridge used to be, then start dancing around wildly, waving the upper set of their arms-legs and squealing angrily.

"I hope the swimmers get here fast enough," said Sneaky, "before the Torwinks can rebuild their bridge." But the stick figures didn't seem to have any such plan. Most of them were staying with their throwing from the lakeshore near where the stream fed into the lake. The swimming Mumwalds were getting much closer, but so long as the Torwinks were confined to the other side of the stream, the swimmers were in no danger. Muscles felt proud that the plan was working so well.

"Look!" said Jester suddenly.

Muscles lifted his club in alarm. "What?" he whispered hoarsely. He and Sneaky looked where Jester was pointing. A few feet east of the stream, the last of three Torwinks was just swinging down onto the path from out of the trees.

"They must have crossed the stream through the aspen tree tops," murmured Jester.

Sage hadn't said anything about this happening. No plan for handling the situation existed. It was up to Muscles to decide what to do. And Muscles was angry—but he also felt a definite thrill, a compelling urge to action.

The mud-daubed Mumwalds slipped a bit farther into the edge of the forest. The Torwinks had given no indication of seeing them. The three Xs were studying the logs the Mumwalds had so easily dragged over to this side of the stream. When the light-weight creatures tried to lift one end of the smallest of the logs, they barely raised it off the ground.

Muscles glanced out at the approaching swimmers. He had decided what he wanted to do. "We just have time," he mumbled, mostly to himself. To his two comrades he said, "Grip your clubs tightly and follow me."

"Wha—" Sneaky started to say, but Muscles was already running toward the Torwinks, who were still facing the stream. Jester and Sneaky swiftly wobbled after him. Little clouds of dust puffed out from under them. The soft dirt on the path absorbed most of the sound of their flapping feet, and the increasing volume of squeaks and squeals as the swimmers got closer covered the rest. The Torwinks probably never knew what hit them. Muscles had raised his club. The other lumbering Mumwalds, abreast of Muscles by then, had caught on and raised theirs. They offered no warning yell. In one motion, each one braked and slammed his club into the junction of an X.

Sneaky and Jester just as quickly started running in the opposite direction. Muscles didn't follow. They turned to see why. They saw him pick up the limp form of the Torwink he had clobbered. He lifted it over his head and tossed it into the middle of the stream. It sank immediately in the rushing water. Before he could pick up another, a horrendous screech came from the throwing Torwinks across the stream and out at the lakeshore. They had just become aware of what was going on. Muscles scooped up his club, shook it defiantly at the screaming Torwinks, and casually trotted toward Jester and Sneaky, who were still dumfounded by what they had witnessed. Muscles pulled up to them with a malignant smile on his face and said, "Well, come on! You two missed half the fun!"

They all backpedaled for a few steps, watching to see what the Torwinks would do. When several disappeared into the trees, the Mumwalds turned and hustled back toward their meeting place. The four swimmers had landed and were almost through the trees. When they met up with the three warriors, they received no greeting. They looked into the flushed face of Muscles—a reddish tint shown right through his fur—and saw exhilaration and bravado. They looked into the glazed stares of Jester and Sneaky and saw shock and horror. But it was no time for explanations. Captain quickly took over, ordering the seven of them to walk swiftly up the path toward the falls. When they were halfway there, two Torwinks, high up in trees, threw three or four rocks at them, but the rocks were small.

"Ah," observed Strongheart. "They can't carry many rocks while they climb, and the ones they can are not big enough to do much damage."

Motherthree sighed. "Whew. That's a relief. That was my last worry."

Sneaky kept beside Motherfive. The good mother's double duty of the night was showing. Her eyelids drooped and her

breathing was heavier than it should have been from the brisk walking pace alone. Sneaky shifted his club to his left hand. With his other hand he gripped Motherfive firmly on the upper arm to help propel her along. He barely heard her mumbled "Thank you."

A few more small stones flitted down at them from high in the trees as they hurried along, but they ignored them. It seemed clear that the Torwinks had no supply of stones on this side of the stream and would not, therefore, be able to keep up any sustained volley, even of small missiles. When the Mumwalds got within fifty yards of the stream, Captain began talking in stride. "We have a big advantage on these vicious creatures. They don't know where we're going, so they don't know where to concentrate an attack. As soon as the path gets to the water, we must all jump in together and swim upstream as fast as possible. We mustn't give them time to mass in the trees before we get into the rock-walled canyon."

"Captain...wait," said Motherfive breathlessly. Captain kept walking but turned a bit sideways to acknowledge that he was waiting for Motherfive to continue. "Wait...stop," she said as she halted. She squatted, resting her sphere on her heels. "I can't...talk and walk...at the same time."

All the Mumwalds stopped. Muscles was irritated. "Well?" he said huffily. Captain frowned at him in the dawn light and stepped back to the tired mother. He gently laid a hand near her top and waited for her to go on. Her top felt unusually warm.

"I think," she said, "we are just about abreast of the slide—you know, the one I used to get down from the cliff above. It shouldn't be far through the forest to the bottom of it."

A small shower of rocks splattered onto the standing Mumwalds. One sharp stone hit Motherfive right on the top. She started to fall backwards off her haunches, but Sneaky was right there to hold her up. Muscles glowered at Captain.

"Ah, I see," said Captain, who hadn't seen the exhausted mother get hit. "Then we could get to the stream the way you did. That would put us right at the mouth of the canyon. We wouldn't have to swim upstream with trees above us at all. Excellent." He looked at Muscles with a smug grin. "Wouldn't you say so, Muscles?"

The irascible warrior lowered his eyelids. "Uh," he grunted, and turned toward the forest.

Minutes later, the Mumwalds were jumping into the stream. They paddled furiously against the light current with Sneaky and Strongheart behind Motherfive helping to push her along, and soon they were all gathered behind the falls. Four of them felt elated. No Torwinks had confronted them on the ground, and the ones in the trees had been seemingly ineffective. Motherfive felt only a profound weariness. Jester and Sneaky were quiet and troubled.

They had witnessed one of their own go far beyond the bounds of self-defense, and they didn't know what to do with that.

15

New Revelations from the Past

It was quite light when they came out into their own valley, but the warming rays of the sun hadn't reached the valley floor. Every Mumwald, from youngest to oldest, was waiting at the passage entrance. Sage, shivering slightly from the morning chill, counted the returning party as they filed out. "One, two, three, four, five, six, seven. Excellent! You have all returned." He looked at the broad smiles of Muscles and Captain. "I take it the rescue mission was a total success."

"It couldn't have gone better," boasted Muscles as he sidled over to Motherfour. She took his free hand in both hers and squeezed it proudly.

Captain said, "It was an excellent plan, Sage. What little opposition we met was virtually harmless, and we didn't have to confront any of the little monsters directly."

Sneaky was sitting by the cliff next to Motherfive, sooth-ingly rubbing her sore left arm, which had taken most of the strain from the brake-stick on the slide. He stopped rubbing and twisted around, looking for Jester. The jokester was standing a couple of steps behind the crowd. His glum face was tilted toward the ground. He did not return Sneaky's stare.

"What's the matter?" mumbled Motherfive. "Keep rub-bing. I like that."

Sneaky silently gazed at Jester for a few more seconds before he turned back to Motherfive. "Uh...oh, nothing." He resumed his massaging rather listlessly, his mind struggling to decide whether he should report what he and Jester and Muscles had done, and what he and Jester had seen Muscles do after that. Apparently Muscles wasn't going to say a thing, though it was his place to.

While he was still mulling over the problem, he heard Sage say, "Let's go have some breakfast, everyone!"

Most of the Mumwalds were once again in an excited state of mind. They pranced and danced and chattered and croaked their way along beside the lake. Jester lagged behind. Sneaky was holding onto Motherfive's arm as she slowly limped along. He glanced back at his comrade, then spoke softly to the good mother beside him. "Can you go on alone?"

She nodded weakly. "I'll try to catch up shortly," he said soothingly. He released her arm and watched her totter along. Motherthree came over, took her arm and said, "I think we'd better have Healer take a look at you."

Sneaky waited for Jester to catch up. The two males fleetingly looked each other in the eye before they turned to stand and stare blankly at the lake. Sneaky spoke first. "What should we do?"

"I don't know," mumbled Jester.

"Muscles was leader and should have reported what we did."

"Yeah."

They stood silently, engrossed in their confused feelings. Suddenly, the loud snap of a twig jerked them to attention.

They spun around to see Stargazer standing a few feet behind them. He was holding a blade of water grass, running his fingers along it. The rest of the Mumwalds were already up to the path.

"Jester? Sneaky?" said Stargazer. "Are you two all right?"

Neither of them spoke.

"I've been watching you two. Neither of you seems to be sharing the excitement and enthusiasm of the moment. There must be a reason."

Sneaky looked at Jester. "Should I tell him?" he muttered.

An almost imperceptible nod of his sphere was all Jester could muster. Once Sneaky got started, the words flew out of his mouth as if they were caged birds exulting in escape. He told of the clubbing of the three Torwinks and of Muscles tossing one of the downed stick figures into the stream. By the time he had finished, both he and Jester had tears welling up in their eyes. Jester began to tremble slightly. Stargazer stepped close and gave both a pat on the forehead. "I am not surprised by this news. But you two shouldn't worry. You were following orders, and you took only the minimal action needed to eliminate the threat."

"Will...will you tell Sage?" asked Sneaky.

Stargazer thought for a moment. "He must be informed. But I confess, I'm not sure what the best way to handle this situation is. For now, let's just go get some cones to eat."

When the three arrived at the wide, low ledge in front of the caves, Sneaky looked around for Motherfive. She wasn't among the crowd. Motherthree slipped away from the others and came up to Sneaky, her eyes showing her worry. "Healer is examining her," she said. "They're in Healer's cave."

Sneaky murmured a thank you and flapped quickly to the third cave. He halted at the entrance. As he peered into the semi-darkness, he saw Healer's dim form hovering over Motherfive, who seemed to be lying on her back. When Healer realized that Sneaky was standing there, she quietly stepped up to him. "I have given her something to make her sleep very deeply for all the rest of the day and perhaps most of the night."

"How is she? What's wrong with her? Just tiredness?"

"The answer to all your questions is the same—I don't know. From what I've heard, she exerted herself far beyond what she is used to. It was unfortunate she had to go back with the rescue party."

"Rest will bring her back to normal then?" said Sneaky.

"We'll hope so." Healer lowered her voice before she continued. "There's one additional problem I haven't mentioned to anyone. But I think you have a right to know because of your special relationship with Motherfive."

The top of Sneaky's sphere suddenly turned quite pink. He shifted his eyes away from Healer and coughed once or twice. "Uh, wh-what's this n-new problem?" he stammered.

"She has a very small but very odd wound on her top. It is so small it couldn't be seen until I pushed aside her fur, and there is almost no blood. But…." She paused to look around at her patient. "But it is very deep. I can't be sure how deep, though, because I didn't want to force it open. Because of where it is, it—"

"Yes, I know," interrupted Sneaky. "I don't know why our tops have to be so tender. I do remember now that a rock thrown from up in a tree hit her as we returned from the lake. It must have had a very sharp point."

"Possibly so. As you know, this kind of wound is extremely unpredictable. We'll just have to see how she is after she comes out of her sleep."

Sneaky didn't answer immediately. Finally, though, he said, "OK…and I think you should tell Sage about that wound."

Healer indicated with a nod that she would.

After breakfast, everyone scattered. Sage retreated to the entrance to his cave, sitting as usual with his back against the cliff. He watched his friends come and go while his aging body soaked up the soothing rays of the early morning sun. His face relaxed, even, perhaps, smiling a bit. It didn't change as Stargazer meandered over and sat next to him.

After several minutes of silence, Sage said, "I know, I know. We still have a cone problem."

"Yes. But that's not why I'm here." Stargazer's voice sounded even more solemn than necessary.

"We aren't going to get back into those infernal 'why' questions, are we?" said Sage, but without rancor.

"I wish that's all I had to talk to you about."

Sage twisted to look at his protégé. "What is it, my son?" He put a palm against Stargazer's side.

"I wonder if that's a sign." The younger Mumwald pointed nearly straight up. An eagle was floating in the air currents above that end of the valley. It looked so harmless in its graceful soaring.

"You are being very evasive," said Sage.

"All right. Here it is. Captain's report about what happened on the rescue mission was incomplete...but it wasn't his fault. He didn't know about something else that happened." And with that introduction, Stargazer told Sneaky's story. When he had finished, Sage sat in stunned silence, his arms hanging limp by his sides. He felt no immediate rush of anger, only a profound sense of something ineffable yet invaluable being irretrievably lost. It was a long time before he spoke, his voice so weak Stargazer could hardly hear him. "I'm at a loss. What should we do? I don't see how I can simply ignore Muscles' action."

"No, we can't do that," said Stargazer with gentle firmness. "Doesn't your memory bring up any wisdom from the past to advise you?"

"I hadn't even thought of searching there." Sage's eyes glazed over as he retreated into his mind. Before very long his arms stiffened, and he pushed himself into a straighter sitting position, leaving his palms pressed against the ledge. "Yes. There is something we should do. It hasn't been done in many, many generations, so I had pushed it far out of my active memory. The last few generations of sages have considered it of historical interest only. It was thought that we would never have to use it again."

"Well...what is it? Some different kind of ceremony or something?"

"Not exactly. It is called a 'trial.' It is a Mumwald gathering at which someone accused of wrongdoing is questioned. And statements are made by others who know something of the misdeed. Then all adults vote on whether the accused is guilty. In early times, only a majority vote was sought. But as Mumwalds became more and more of one mind about how they should behave, the outcomes were always unanimous."

"And what happened if the accused was found guilty?"

"A large catalog of misdeeds and their corresponding punishments exists."

"What was the punishment for killing another creature—but not a Mumwald?"

Sage shuddered visibly. Almost inaudibly, he said, "It depended on how and why the killing was done. In the earliest days, the worst of the killers were forced out into the lake and made to plunge over the falls. Later...aha!" Sage's face suddenly became alert. He brought his hands together in front of his mouth. "So that's it! That memory was buried back there with crime and punishment. No wonder I couldn't find the answer earlier."

"Whoa! What are you talking about?"

"Yes, yes, my boy, you have a right to be confused. You see, I just recalled the reason why the tunnel down to the falls was hewn through the rock long ago."

"Hey, I'll bet I get it. Our forefathers sent killers away through the tunnel rather than making them go over the falls?"

"Exactly. And they called that punishment 'banishment.' No one ever heard back from any of the Mumwalds who were sent down."

"Hmm. That could be worse than being put to death if the one banished fell into the hands of vicious creatures."

"I suppose so. But by the time they started that, very few had to be sent away."

"That makes me curious about something. When you first revealed the legend of the secret passage, the story spoke of explorers starting down the tunnel, getting scared, and retreating.

"Why didn't they know from the tradition that Mumwalds had carved the tunnel in the first place and knew where it went?"

"Oh my, yes, that is an interesting question. Let me see. My memory must have a link that explains that. Mmmm. We sages are fed so many stories and thoughts it is hard to bring them all up." Sage was quite perky now, as his attention was drawn away from the confused feelings stirred up by Muscles. His eyes danced as he plunged back into his mind. "Ah, it is quite simple. Those explorers found the tunnel opening and went exploring before they had mentioned it to the sage of that time. Upon their return, they made up the poem I recited...you remember...'fear in each sphere'?"

"Of course."

"The sage then let them have their fun telling their story and even entered it into the tradition. That sage never did tell those Mumwalds why the tunnel was there. He encouraged them to think of it as a possible escape route to be used only in emergencies. It was that memory—from rather recent times—that I dredged up before. This new one had remained hidden from me until just now." He turned toward Stargazer and gave his young friend a warm smile. "You will find, too, that not everything comes back to you when you would like."

Stargazer nodded in understanding. He felt a strong bond between himself and this warm, wise old fellow next to him.

"Well!" spoke Sage, with authority now. "Please summon Captain for me."

Captain arranged for a trial to be conducted that evening as soon as the shadow of the western cliff covered the theater at the eastern end of the valley. Sage had decided that the cool of the evening was the best time for this gathering. When Captain informed Muscles of the proceedings, the newly designated defendant was at first furious, as expected. Motherfour, however, was seen taking him by the hand and leading him down the forest path later in the morning. At lunch, Muscles' disposition was no grumpier than usual. The mood of the little society of Mumwalds that afternoon as they awaited this new experience was a curious one. It could best be described by the word *pensive*. It was all so new to them; they didn't know enough to be apprehensive, yet they realized that a most serious matter was to be dealt with. One other fact in their lives added a twinge of foreboding to their mood. Healer reported that Motherfive was still sleeping under the influence of the herb she had given her, but the sick one's breathing was now in shallow, rapid puffs.

Through the afternoon, the more Sage thought about the situation the less uncomfortable he got. He didn't like what had happened, of course, but he could easily imagine circumstances that would have made the attack on the Torwinks warranted by self-defense, even Muscles' extra action of throwing the one in the water. He began to believe that the catalog of crimes and punishments would have no application that evening. He even began to wonder if he had been hasty in calling for a trial, but then he decided that at least it would give them a chance to clear the air of suspicion and misinformation. By suppertime, he had talked himself into quite a cheerful mood.

16

The Trial

That evening Healer stayed in her cave with Motherfive while all other Mumwalds met at the theater. Sage started the event without fanfare. Briefly, in a businesslike manner, he went over why they had gathered and he outlined the procedure.

Muscles was the first to testify. He stood on the lowest level, facing the others. His rigid arms were pointed straight down, his fists clenched. As he talked, his eyes darted nervously from Mumwald to Mumwald. His voice did not falter, but it was slightly higher pitched than usual. "Sneaky and Jester and I...we were just standing at the edge of the path waiting for the swimmers. All of a sudden, Jester saw these three Torwinks on our side of the bridge. Sage hadn't told us what to do in a case like this. I decided we needed to take care of them—wouldn't do to have them that close. So we took out running with our clubs ready. The little devils never did see us. They were studying the bridge we had torn down, and there was a lot of racket from the other Torwinks across the stream down at the lake. We ran up to those three and bashed their heads in. We started to run back, but out of the corner of my eye I saw one of the Torwinks move. Since the clubbing hadn't worked, I picked him up and threw him in the stream. He didn't even try to swim or wade out—just sank like a stone. Then I turned again and ran to catch up with Sneaky and Jester."

Muscles' eyes continued to shift back and forth. His fingers started clenching, then unclenching, again and again.

Stargazer twisted toward Motherone and whispered in her ear. "That's not quite the way I heard it from Sneaky."

"You mean he lied?" she whispered back, incredulous.

Stargazer rocked his sphere in a nod.

"But that has to be a...a deliberate...."

Stargazer nodded again and hissed the undesirable word, "*Sin.*" He pressed his lips tightly together as he turned back to watch what happened next.

Sage was talking privately in low tones to Muscles. Soon he motioned for the strong one to sit down between Strongheart and Captain. Sneaky was called down to testify. He kept his eyes fixed on a spot directly in front of him on the first ledge. "It...ah...pretty much happened...ah...the way Muscles there told it. I...ah...don't have anything to add...and neither does Jester. He asked me to say that." Without being formally dismissed, he quickly waddled back to his seat.

Sage didn't try to stop him. The halting, frightened manner of Sneaky's testimony went unacknowledged. The old one stood up, breathed deeply of the cool evening air, and smiled at the assembly. He was the perfect picture of self-satisfaction, for everything was proceeding smoothly toward the ending he had imagined that afternoon. "We have heard the testimony of those involved," he said confidently, "and we should now be ready to vote on—"

Two highly audible gasps interrupted him. He looked up at the row from which Stargazer and Motherone were staring at him with disbelieving faces. Warily, and with a hint of

impatience, he said, "Did one of you want to say something before we vote?"

"Er, well, yes," said Stargazer. "With all due respect, I would suggest that we are moving a bit too fast. Shouldn't we have…er, shouldn't we open the proceedings up for questions or comments from anyone?"

"For crying out loud," said Muscles. "You've heard from the three of us that were involved. What more do you want?"

Sage moved quickly to keep control. "Hush, hush, now. We must move in an orderly manner, according to the tradition." He paused. He had heard Sneaky's first version of the story and knew very well that Sneaky and Jester had felt then that Muscles was not at all justified in throwing the injured Torwink in the water. He was perfectly willing, however, to accept without question the possibility that those two had begun to see the situation from a different perspective and were now accepting Muscles' version. Doing this would bring the assembly to a quick, decisive, and above all, positive ending. He had to think of some way to head off any questions by Stargazer and Motherone.

Before he could continue, though, a voice spoke from an unexpected quarter. "Yup, my good man, I do have a question. Yup, I do," said Dumbell, his eyes wide and his eyebrows raised. A closemouthed grin stretched across his face.

Sage felt trapped. He had tried many times to shut off Dumbell when the slow-thinking one got a notion in his mind, and none of his attempts had worked. "Please go ahead, Dumbell," he said resignedly.

"Yup. Thanks, old boy. You see, this morning I was sittin' behind a big tree thinkin' stupid thoughts like you all think I think." He paused to chuckle at his little joke. No one else laughed with him. "Yup, OK, so Sneaky and Jester came along and didn't see me. They was on the other side of the tree. They talked a lot about this fight thing. They sounded awful sad—and scared, especially scared. They was sayin' that Muscles there…hey, Muscles, my good man." Dumbell stopped to wave at the frowning defendant. "Yes sir, I know how you like to fight, Mr. Muscles. Yup, I sure do. And Sneaky and Jester, they said you didn't need to throw that little feller in the drink. You just did it out of meanness. Whoops, they didn't say that last thing, about meanness. That was from me just now. Yup, that's what I think." And he quit without ever asking a question.

Stargazer again whispered to Motherone. "Thank Great Maker that Dumbell said all that instead of one of us. If we'd said it, the North Wind would've broken loose all over for sure." Other Mumwalds were whispering hoarsely and excitedly to neighbors.

Spouting words furiously and incoherently, Muscles joggled over to Sage, waving one arm wildly and pointing up at Dumbell with the other. Sage unthinkingly gave Muscles a light push back toward his seat and raised his own arms, holding his hands with palms outward in front of his face asking for quiet. Muscles scowled but grudgingly backed up to his seat.

"Children, children!" Sage cried shrilly. "Please! Order, please!" Gradually, quiet came over the group. When he had everyone's attention, Sage looked squarely at Dumbell and said, "Thank you for that contribution, Dumbell. However, I think you must have misunderstood some of what you heard. We must consider—"

"Sage, how can you say that!" Motherone was on her feet, almost shrieking. "Others of us have heard what Dumbell reported. You must let us discuss this matter so we can get at the truth!" As she plopped back down, her whole sphere was shaking. Stargazer clutched her hand and squeezed it tightly.

Sage was so dumfounded by this outburst that he could only stare at the impertinent mother. Muscles couldn't stand the hesitation. In a menacing growl, he said, "You have the truth, lady. You just don't want to believe it. You heard what I said—and what Sneaky said. Now keep quiet!"

"I...I...." stuttered Sage.

"We'd better take a break and go cool off in the lake," said Motherthree.

Sage glanced at Muscles' tense face and bright pink top. "I...don't think we'd better do that," he said, realizing the danger of releasing the wolf among the lambs in open pasture—even though he knew nothing of wolves and lambs. He looked at Stargazer. The expression of fervent determination on the next sage's face gave the old leader strength. Speaking with quiet resolution, he said, "We must see this through, wherever it may take us. Sneaky or Jester, would one of you care to comment on Dumbell's remarks?"

Sneaky didn't move. Jester was holding his hands over his eyes. Slipping off his seat, Stargazer walked over to Sneaky, took him by the hand, and led him down to the front of the group. When Stargazer tried to draw away his hand, Sneaky wouldn't let go. Stargazer relaxed and waited for his friend to speak.

Avoiding Muscles' fierce glare, Sneaky said, "I guess I should have added something to what Muscles said a while ago. Jester and I weren't sure we should, but...well, you see, after we clubbed our Torwinks, we saw them all collapse like crumpled spiders. We turned and ran. But we didn't go far because we quickly realized Muscles wasn't with us. When we turned to see why, he was leaning over to pick up his Torwink. The Torwink was still a crumpled mass. I doubt if he'd even blinked his eye.

"We didn't understand why Muscles did what he did, but he was our leader. And we didn't have a chance to stop him. We got this awful feeling inside us and didn't know what to do about it."

As he spoke, Captain and Strongheart, flanking Muscles, felt the vibrations of the strong one's arms. Without realizing that the other had done the same thing, each one firmly grasped Muscles' arm closest to him. It felt like they were holding back a young spruce tree that had been bent far over and was trying to spring back into its natural position.

Motherthree asked, "Were you afraid to say all that earlier?"

"Yes."

"Did anyone threaten you about testifying?" said Stargazer.

"N-no, not exactly. We could just feel...." He couldn't finish. Tears started streaming down his white fur. Sage signaled Stargazer to take Sneaky back to his seat.

"Muscles, would you care to respond to these new developments?" Sage deliberately approached Muscles in a matter-of-fact manner, hoping to defuse the terrible temper that everyone could feel.

The strategy worked. Muscles shook off the grips of his two guards and stood up. Instead of turning to face the crowd, he spoke out to the meadow and forest and lake. "You bet I do! All right, maybe that dirty little bag of sticks didn't move much. I still thought he deserved to be tossed in the water. I don't see anything wrong with that!"

"If you don't see anything wrong with it," said Strongheart, "then why didn't you admit it in the first place?"

"Cause I didn't think some of you sissies would understand!"

The assembly immediately erupted in an uproar of shouts and insults. Sage and Stargazer were unsuccessfully pleading for calm when Healer wobbled out of the trees on the forest path. One of the mothers cried above the din. "Healer! Oh, no!" Everyone immediately shut up. They watched the nurse hustle up to Sage and whisper to him. As he listened, Sage's arms drooped to his side. His knees began to shake. Healer helped him to the lowest ledge, where he sat with eyes fixed on the ground.

Sneaky watched them. Without a word, tears flowed anew from his eyes.

Healer stepped back from Sage and addressed the assembly. "Sage has asked me to report my message to you all. I'm deeply saddened to tell you that Motherfive stopped breathing in her sleep a bit ago. She lies dead in my cave. Her unborn child is not far enough along to try to save." A heavy silence engulfed the Mumwalds. Captain scooted off his seat and shuffled over to Sage. The two spoke in whispers for a few moments; then Captain backed up beside Healer and announced, "We will go ahead with a Ceremony of the Star for Motherfive later this evening. For now, the assembly is dismissed." The Mumwalds slowly separated to wander back to their caves. Stargazer and Motherone helped Sneaky along the path.

The ceremony that night wasn't successful. They lay in the theater half the night, but the Wondrous Star didn't come. Finally, Sage rose and led them in silence toward their caves.

Captain and Strongheart stopped at the lakeshore where they had left Motherfive's body earlier. They couldn't let it drift over the falls yet, so they towed it across the water to a special spot at the far southwestern edge of the lake. There the Mumwalds had prepared a special repository for corpses awaiting the Wondrous Star. Two large boulders lay naturally close to each other, partly on the bank and partly submerged in the water. In the water between the ends of the boulders, Mumwalds had piled stones loosely to form a wall that came above the surface and kept a body from floating out of the enclosure. Fresh spruce branches earlier had been spread from one boulder top to the other to provide protection from the sun for the corpse. Into this temporary sanctuary the two males gently placed Motherfive.

Near the caves was a large, flat stone with a hollowed out, bowl-shaped hole in its top. Sage stopped by this stone and stood there while the others plodded past him. As Jester passed, Sage took his arm and pulled him aside. "You take the first watch," Sage said.

Jester nodded, climbed up on the stone, and lay down with his back in the rounded hole. Mumwalds would take turns lying there each night until one of them spotted the Wondrous Star taking the soul of Motherfive away. There was no danger that the watching Mumwald would roll off the stone when he or she got drowsy. The hole in the stone took care of that. And a strong incentive to stay awake was the punishment for going to sleep—isolation in one's cave for three days without speaking with anyone. They knew that if the star hadn't come by the end of the tenth night, the soul of Motherfive was lost to the North Wind. But that was a long time away. For now, Jester settled into the hole sadly, yet not without hope. The others went to their caves for sleep. During the rest of the night, Mothertwo, then Lazy, took their turns watching for the star. It didn't come.

Word spread the next morning that Sage wanted another assembly fairly soon, when the valley was half full of sun. Leaving Sneaky in the care of Jester and Climber with Mothersix, Stargazer and Motherone started for the theater early.

They didn't want to hurry. When they were far enough away from the others, Motherone asked, "Did Sage consult with you about what he was going to do at this assembly?"

"No, I haven't even spoken with him since before the Ceremony of the Star last night."

"That worries me. Doesn't it you?"

Stargazer nodded his sphere as he said, "Greatly." He stooped to pick up a cone off the ground. It was blotched with the orange fungus. "Funny, I'd almost forgotten what started this whole terrible chain of events. It was only four days ago that the first bad cone came to our attention."

"Yes. That and the Torwinks' odd behavior have had frightening consequences." She walked on quietly for a moment, then said, "Stargazer, am I wrong, or are we becoming more and more enmeshed in this...this sin business?"

"Humph. You certainly aren't wrong. It is strange, though, how much more forcefully sin seems to be taking hold in some of us than in others."

"True. But I suspect that all of us are letting loose of feelings toward others that could easily erupt in sinful behavior. Muscles' viciousness is obvious, but think about Sneaky. Surely he harbors thoughts of revenge against the Torwinks for the death of his mate and their child within her. And I'll bet he also feels profound disgust at Muscles, not only for that oaf's violent streak but also because of his lying."

They had just come to the lake. Stargazer veered off the path, leading Motherone to the cool water's edge. They sat on rocks, letting the gentle waves lap the ends of their feet. "Circumstances beyond our control put us in a situation that aroused sin in us," mused Stargazer. "Then new situations beyond our control arose, deepening our predicament. And sin in one begets more sin in another. It *is* becoming very complicated."

Motherone sniffed a chuckle. "For many generations our sages have been telling us what a perfect life we have, with peace and harmony for all. Will you be able to pass on that message when you are sage?"

Stargazer flicked water with his foot. "Hardly." He paused. "You know, I'm sure Sage would say we are regressing. But I wonder. This may sound awfully strange, but the last day or two have you been feeling some kind of...of excitement? I mean, in spite of the terrible things that have been happening, have you felt...hmm, how can I say it...that your life has been expanding, that your experience has even been enhanced? Am I making any sense?"

"Not much. But go on." Motherone's eyebrows hinted at a frown, not because of what Stargazer was saying but because she was remembering something Healer had mentioned in a nurturing-the-young session one time when no males—not even young ones—were present. The good mother decided once again not to reveal her memory.

"When things are rolling along smoothly in our valley, and there are no significant clashes or conflicts with anybody or anything, doesn't life get a bit dull? Could it be that the more variety of feelings we allow ourselves to experience, the more unusual circumstances we allow ourselves to dive into, the richer our lives are? Even when these feelings and circumstances bring discord into our lives? Don't you feel a stimulating challenge in trying to form a new harmony out of the discordant elements we now face? It's almost as if...as if our life before all this trouble was...hmm, I'm not sure...yeah, that's it! Trivial! We had reduced our lives to maintaining a trivial level of existence! Wouldn't you agree?"

"Maybe—at least as long as the discord doesn't get out of hand. Too much of that could lead to a breakdown in the basic traditions we live by. I mean...well, we need some order or we'll end up in chaos." She paused, a new frown forming. "Stargazer," she said in a hushed tone, "are you suggesting...my goodness, I hope not...but do you think we need to bring sin back into our lives or have tragedies happen to us in order to lead full lives?"

"Good grief, I don't know. Am I saying that?"

Just then, from the path a voice called. "Hey, you two, hustle your stubby legs to the theater. The sun's about halfway."

* * *

All the Mumwalds except one were seated on the ledges.

Captain looked concerned. "Did anyone see Sage on his way here?"

The Mumwalds twisted from side to side. They looked at each other, puzzled. Here was yet another wonder. Sage had never been late before. Suddenly, a "pssst" from the crowd caused everyone to look up. Sage, his sphere tilted forward and one hand clutching a sturdy walking stick, was emerging from the forest, halfway between the two paths. He plodded slowly through the meadow, not caring what he crushed under his broad feet. He looked like a heavy barge being poled along a reed-filled canal, sweeping everything in its way under its massive hull.

Captain, thinking the old leader might be sick, rose to go help him. Sage looked up, lifted a hand to signal Captain to stay put, and dragged on to the front of the assembly. Mothertwo reached down and took hold of Mischief. This was no time for any kind of trouble, accidental or not.

"I'm sorry I'm late," said Sage in a shaky, solemn voice.

New streaks of black laced his fur. He leaned heavily on his walking stick. "I did not sleep last night. I have wandered alone in the forest since daybreak. My spirit is heavy." He paused to look from side to side at the assembled Mumwalds, his eyelids droopy.

"We have a food problem. We tried to solve it by using Climber, only to lose the blessed Ancientone in the attack by the eagle. Then we tried to solve it according to the Way of the Chipmunk. In so doing, we were attacked for reasons we cannot understand.

And worst of all, we have lost one of our beloved mothers and the unborn she carried. Perhaps I was wrong in choosing Motherfive to go on the mission."

Sneaky's round body jerked; his hands shook involuntarily.

Sage went on. "But she had no young ones at this time. If any mother had to be lost, it was better for her not to have young. I took a risk with Motherthree—but if she were lost, her Rammer and Roller are old enough to adapt to the loss without undue trauma. Now, though, I will never be the same, having chosen Motherfive to go to her death." Sage's voice was so shaky that the others thought he would break down and cry.

Motherone looked at Stargazer and whispered, "Where is this leading? How's he going to deal with Muscles?"

Stargazer merely raised his eyebrows.

Suddenly Sage shook himself. He took a deep breath. A strange, hard look came into his eyes. "My friends!" His voice boomed now, startling his audience. He jabbed the walking stick into the air. "Prepare yourselves for the Way of the Eagle! We have no other choice before us. Our food problem is still with us. We have lost two loved ones, one because of the horrible Torwinks. We have a double reason now to return to their territory. We will make them pay for Motherfive's death, and we will destroy as many of them as necessary in order to allow us safe passage to get untainted cones. We shall prevail!"

"Whoopee!" Muscles was on his feet, dancing crazily in circles. But all the mother Mumwalds absorbed Sage's words in stony, awed silence. Motherfour tugged at Muscles' arm and pulled him back to his seat. Sage had one last thing to say. "We will need a word for what we are about to do. We will call it *war*."

17

Dumbell and Dissension

Sage had to sit down. None of the other Mumwalds moved or spoke. A few began fantasizing about different ways they would attack their enemies in this new event called war. Others thought ahead to the possibility that Mumwalds would be hurt, and more very likely would die. Still others tried to imagine what it would feel like to kill another creature deliberately. Only four of the Mumwalds—Stargazer, Motherone, Sneaky and Strongheart—brooded about the aborted trial of Muscles, yet each of them felt that openly raising that issue at this moment would be totally fruitless and might even be dangerous.

All of this somber thinking was finally too much for Dumbell. He began to sing quietly.

Oh, I wish I was a fishy in the lake,
Oh, I wish I was a fishy in the lake,

125

I'd go swimmin' in my nudey,
Without my furry suity.
Oh, I wish I was a fishy in the lake.

He paused after that verse. Even he was smart enough to know that such a song was out of place at a time like this. He fully expected a scolding from Sage. He didn't care. For him, even in his mental dimness, the sadness wrought by the mere thought of war was numbing and overwhelming. He had to get his mind off it.

Curiously, no one spoke. Not even Sage. When Dumbell had started singing, they had all raised their heads. The humor of the song brought a touch of lightness to their minds; a dash of hope seeped into even the most weary and worried souls.

When it became clear that Dumbell wasn't going to sing more, Sage said softly, "Go on, Dumbell. Sing the rest for us."

Dumbell was wide-eyed but otherwise expressionless. After a moment he clapped his hands together and said, "Glad to, my good man. Yup. Shall I come forward?"

"Please do."

Dumbell wobbled down to the front of the assembly. He was taking himself very seriously, adjusting his stance several times and trying to get just the right expression on his face. As he began singing, he flapped his feet and twisted and swayed his body in rhythm with his song.

Oh, I wish I was a chippy in the woods,
Oh, I wish I was a chippy in the woods,
I would hop upon a twig.
And dance a little jig,
Oh, I wish I was a chippy in the woods.

Several Mumwalds chuckled. Mischief patted his hands together in delight. Dumbell grinned widely and went on.

Oh, I wish I was a little spot of mud,
Oh, I wish I was a little spot of mud,
I'd get flat into a pie,
And fly splat in someone's eye,
Oh, I wish I was a little spot of mud.

More Mumwalds joined in the chuckling. Jester, suddenly catching the mood and snapping out of the depression he'd been in since the rescue mission, shouted out, "Hey, who knows what grows outward but never upward?"

"Not one of your riddles!" said Lazy with a good-humored groan.

"Your tummy?" squealed Mischief.

Jester rolled his eyes downward to look at the middle of his sphere. He smiled. "That, young sir, was an insult—but all too true. However, it wasn't the right answer! Who knows?"

No one said anything, so Jester gleefully cried, "Gotcha on this one. It's ripples made by a rock thrown in the lake!"

"Boooo!"

"Get him outta here!"

"Roarrrk, roarrrk!"

"Hey, since you liked that one so much, here's another. Why don't we swim on a full stomach?"

"Because it's easier to swim on water," said Lazy with a yawn.

"Absolutely right! An extra spruce cone for that Mumwald!"

Motherone turned to Stargazer. "Can you believe the mood they're getting into?" she said disgustedly.

Stargazer twisted from side to side and quietly replied, "But it's exactly what Sage wanted. Just watch him use this and build on it."

Sage rose, raising his stick as a call for attention. "I thank you all for these light moments. It is just what we needed. We should be ready now to get down to business."

Stargazer nudged the disgusted mother beside him.

Sage went on. "The Way of the Eagle will include two missions into the valley of the Torwinks. The first we will do at a time when no Torwinks will bother us. It will be a mission of revenge and of rendering the Torwinks incapable of fighting. The second we will do when danger of attack by Torwinks is past. It will be a mission to gather cones."

"Wait, wait!" broke in Muscles worriedly. "You say the Torwinks aren't going to bother us? How will we get close enough to them to get revenge for Motherfive's death?"

"Think, my impatient Muscles. What have we learned that Torwinks do not like—apparently can't tolerate well at all?"

"Uh...uh, water, I guess."

"Yes! So all we do is wait for a gloriously rainy day. Rain water should be as distasteful to the Torwinks as lake or stream water. Perhaps their bodies are so thin that a little chill goes right through them."

"Wonderful thinking, my good man. Yup, your brain is bigger than the biggest rock in our valley."

Sage smiled at Dumbell. "I hope my brain is not also as hard as that rock."

Motherone and Stargazer exchanged glances. Most of the rest of the crowd relaxed even more. Sage went on to tell them how they could hurt the Torwinks without even seeing them. When the meeting broke up, many of the round creatures leapt from their seats and headed excitedly for the lake. Motherone and Stargazer simply stood at their places and were soon joined by Sneaky and Strongheart. No words were spoken. With solemn faces, the four moved in unison down the ledges to confront Sage, who was giving detailed instructions to Captain.

Sage dismissed Captain with a pat on the side and turned to the four, a confident smile still on his face. "Ahh, Stargazer, thank you for your silent support during the meeting. I was afraid that you or some of your...." He paused to look Sneaky and Strongheart in the eye. He avoided the troubled mother. "...your friends might choose to question my decisions. That would have been extremely disturbing."

Motherone burst in. "How could you ignore Muscles? What are you going to do about him? His behavior has to be dealt with! And what have you ordered us to do to the Torwinks? We can't afford—"

Sage put up a hand and said forcefully, "Please, good mother, give me a chance to explain." He waited a moment to see if he was going to be interrupted by another outburst. When he wasn't, he continued. "I am very aware that we have left the matter of Muscles unresolved. But we are facing a crisis. The trial turned out to be a divisive thing, I admit. I never should have tried to conduct one. For that, I apologize. What we need now is unity. We must deal with Motherfive's death and the food problem immediately. And we can't do that effectively if we are split into two or more camps. You saw what happened last night. If Healer hadn't come along, I dare say we would have had a fight—I mean a physical fight—on our hands, and some of you probably would have been involved. We must put Muscles' behavior behind us, for now at least. Perhaps in the future...."

"But, what about...how can we...what will happen...?" Motherone sputtered angrily.

"I think what she and the rest of us want to say is something like this," said Stargazer. "Muscles has sinned grievously, to put it bluntly. And now we are taking on a revenge mission!"

Sage winced at that but didn't break in.

"If we let Muscles go unpunished and if we deliberately try to harm other creatures, then what are we saying to our young—and even to us adults? Does the wisdom of the ages say that we may condone sin under certain conditions?"

"And you can bet Muscles will kill again and again, if we let him," said Sneaky. "I know. I saw the look on his face when he turned from throwing the Torwink in the stream."

"Why do we have to act so quickly?" asked Strongheart. "Why can't we stop for a day or two and think about all this and discuss it?"

Sage jammed his walking stick against the ledge. "You saw what happened when we tried to discuss the matter at the trial! There is no reason to think that we could do better in another day or two. I had to make the hard decisions— alone. And I did. And that's that, gentlemen and lady. The matter of sin will have to wait."

Stargazer shook his sphere. "Then we will just sink deeper and deeper into the mire."

Sage gazed deeply into his pupil's eyes. A slight droop in his own eyes and at the corners of his mouth softened his expression. "I see no other choice." He turned and walked slowly away, poling with his stick.

18

Revenge Mission

Brief thunderstorms came every afternoon for the next several days. What the Mumwalds needed, however, was an overcast day that promised hours of rain. The four dissenters talked often and long among themselves, but they could find no way out of the trap they felt they were in. Ingrained in them was a deep loyalty to Sage and to Mumwald society; that feeling persisted strongly even though they thought that Sage was leading that society down an unwise and unsafe path. They simply could not bring themselves to foment trouble for Sage. Besides, they could not come up with a reasonable alternative for solving the food problem without re-entering the territory of the Torwinks, and they understood the need for incapacitating the Torwinks and the wisdom of Sage's plea for unity if that was the only solution.

Most of the Mumwalds spent considerable time at new activities. Each one acquired a solid club, and they practiced whacking rocks and trees and sparring with each other. They practiced throwing rocks, too. One day as they were mock attacking each other—war games, they called them—Motherthree had an idea. From several trees she tore branches that were large enough to be sturdy but were still pliable. She broke them off to be a little more than a foot long, then wove them into a flat, matlike square. One stick across the middle, a bit longer than the others, was not drawn tight, so that on one side of the mat a Mumwald could get his fingers under that stick and use it as a handle. Then a Mumwald could hold the mat out in front or above him or wherever he needed to in order to ward off blows of

either club or rock. It was an ingenious device. Sage named it *shield* and gratefully acknowledged its usefulness in this new activity called war.

On the fifth day after Motherfive's ceremony, the morning began bright and clear as usual. By midmorning, however, huge thunderclouds were massing closer and closer together; by noon, a slow, steady drizzle began seeping from the low, solid gray blanket of clouds that had formed.

Captain was lunching with Sage in the latter's cave. "This is our day, Captain," said the old leader. "It will be wet the rest of the afternoon. Call your group together and be on your way."

Captain munched on the remnants of a cone and threw a few spruce needles into his mouth for added flavor. "I'm sure

everyone realizes this is the day." He went to the mouth of the cave. Oddly, he didn't feel like getting soaked yet. Staying just out of the rain, he croaked loudly three times.

Lazy and Muscles were the first two to come dripping into the cave. Soon, Motherthree, Jester, Sneaky, and Strong-heart followed. During the preceding days Sage had privately talked with Stargazer, Strongheart, and Sneaky and had finally convinced them that the latter two, regardless of their feelings, should go along on the mission for revenge, not so much to help against Torwinks but to help Captain control Muscles. Stargazer, as sage-in-training, was not to be put at risk, and Dumbell was too unpredictable. Sage didn't want to send any female this time. Another loss of a member of that sex and the delicate balance that kept their population steady might be irreparably upset. Yet the gray fur of the female had been a great advantage before and might be again. Mother-three would have to go.

"This is it," said Captain to the assemblage. "We'll get our clubs and shields and, if all goes well, we should be back by dark."

"Go then, and do your work well." Confident though he was, a shiver went through Sage. He had never before commanded any Mumwald to go forth to do harm on purpose to any other creature except the eagle. Now he was asking his fellow creatures to do something that should, if his reckoning was right, mean either a slow, agonizing death for the Torwinks or a forced move from their valley home. There would be no joyful sending off of this revenge party.

Out into the rain and down through the passage the force of seven marched. As expected, they encountered no Tor-winks after they passed through the falls and began floating down the stream. A new bridge had been constructed across the stream, but with the steady drizzle the Mumwalds felt secure in ignoring it. Besides, they knew now that Torwinks could cross the stream easily by swinging from branch to branch in the aspen trees. The Mumwalds waded out of the water and hurried down the path to the lake. No Torwinks there, either.

"All right," said Captain. "Everyone into the water."

The Mumwalds laid their shields on the shore and waded into the lake. A hard rain shower burst down on them. Lightning crackled and thunder rumbled through their spheres. They went to work with their hands and clubs, tearing the stems of the lily pads loose from the shallow lake bottom. For a distance of ten feet out from shore they cleared the water of lilies. Many plants grew farther out, but the Torwinks had no way to get to them. The loose lily pads were pushed through the remaining live ones, which formed a barricade that prevented the loose ones from floating back to the edge of the lake.

The job of making inaccessible what they thought to be the Torwinks' only food supply took longer than expected. When they were finally done, they gathered on the shore by the boulder field. Captain said, "Well done. Now the Torwinks will begin to go hungry." He looked at the sky. "With the heavy clouds and rain, we have only a short time of good daylight left."

Lazy sat down on a small rock.

Muscles sneered at him. "Come on, Lazy, our work isn't done yet."

"Go soak your fur," grumbled Lazy.

"What do you think I've been doing all afternoon? If you'd worked a little harder, maybe we'd—"

Captain broke in. "We have more to do than quibble. We're all tired. And we need to explore this side of the valley on our way back. Maybe we'll find something interesting to report."

They retrieved their shields and started up the path by the boulder field. At the north end of that field the path entered a thick grove of aspen. The path seemed to lead more toward the steeply sloped mountainside than the falls. Suddenly they came out of the trees. They stopped immediately, huddled in a tight mass. Before them, rising out of the ground, were little clouds of what seemed to be fog. As they eased closer, they saw that the fog was coming out of two pools within a few feet of each other. And the ground! The closer they got to the pools, the warmer the ground felt! The fog began to drift over them. Motherthree said, "What is this?"

"No big deal," said Muscles. "It's just like the fog that rises out of the ground or lake in our valley once in a while."

"But this fog is so warm!" said the mother. "We don't have anything like it."

"It isn't fog, then," said Jester. "If we don't have anything like it, then we don't have a name for it."

"All right. All right," said Captain, exasperated. "Some of you are grumpy enough for...I don't know what. We'll tell Sage about this stuff, OK? He'll either know what it is, or he'll give it a name."

Through breaks in the fog they could see that the mountainside directly behind the two pools was actually a low cliff. They came up beside the southernmost pool. It wasn't water—just gurgling, sloshy mud. Bubbles popped open at the surface. A large bubble, as big as a half-grown Mumwald, oozed out of the mush and burst, splattering mud on the watchers.

"Ouch!" cried Jester. "That mud is hotter than a rock on the hottest summer day." He backed away, quickly followed by the others.

"Very strange," murmured Captain. "Let's look at the other pool."

The warm, misty fog coming out of the other pool was thicker than that coming from the mud pot. The rain was coming down very lightly, with little wind. The fog stayed close to the ground and spread out along the base of the cliff. The murky cloud was too thick to see through. Coming right up to the edge of the second pool, the Mumwalds gasped. It was filled with the most beautiful emerald water they had ever seen. Even with the ripples from the raindrops, they could see far down into the crystal-clear water. Strongheart stuck the tip of a webbed foot into the water. "Yeow!"

Dropping his club and shield, he lifted the foot and held it in his hands, hopping backwards on his other foot. Captain shoved his shield against Strongheart's arm to help him keep his balance.

"I would say, without really knowing," said Jester drily, "that Strongheart found the water to be hot, too."

As the others gathered around Strongheart, Muscles began inching his way toward the cliff through the fog between the pools. Without warning, the light rain stopped pelting his top. After another step or two the fog thinned considerably, but the pale light of the ending day still grew gloomier, as if he'd stepped under a shadow. He looked up. Through the gentle swirls of light fog he could dimly see rock above him. He had walked under an overhang of the cliff. It formed a natural shelter, warmed by the hot pools. The heat almost choked him—but it occurred to him that such a heated sanctuary might be just what the Torwinks would like.

He took another step forward and suddenly felt himself standing on something very soft. Bending his sphere forward, he tried to see what he had stepped onto. He couldn't tell. Squatting, he rubbed his hand across a furry surface. He jerked to an upright position. Now that his eyes were more used to the shadowy light, he saw only a few feet in front of him two stout sticks standing vertically a couple of feet apart, wedged between floor and ceiling. Stretched between the poles were two more pieces of the furry floor coverings. Muscles' mouth opened in horror.

Then, as he turned his head slowly, he saw slight, dim stick shapes lying and sitting deathly still in the gloom. Right by the pool, where the heat was greatest, was a mother with two young. Muscles saw that the one eye of each Torwink was focused on him. "Aaargh!" he roared, raising his club and shield and methodically starting forward. Before he could advance more than two steps, however, Strongheart, limping only slightly, and Captain burst through the fog shroud. Each grabbed one of Muscles' arms. Shrieks and squeals and squeaks shattered the eerie silence. The shelter burst into life. A volley of little rocks and a shower of dirt fell on the three invaders. Muscles shouted hysterically, "Let me go! Can't you see! Let me at 'em, you fools!" Captain and Strongheart jerked backwards on Muscles and hastily pulled him out through the fog.

When the three were safely back with their comrades, Muscles twisted free from the grip of the others. He waved his club and shield wildly, sputtering incoherently for half a minute. The other six stood sideways and formed a wall between him and the Torwink shelter. They held their shields toward the overhang to fend off the scattering of missiles that flew out of the fog. Finally, Muscles calmed to the point that he could speak. "Didn't you idiots see?" he yelled. "Didn't you see what you were walking on? Didn't you see what was stretched between those sticks? Why did you pull me back?"

"Whoa…hold on…calm down," said Captain. "What are you talking about?"

"Dummy!" shouted Muscles. "You were walking on the skins of our kin! And…and…that must have been Ancientone's skin that was stretched out in two pieces! How could you drag me out of there! I'd have—"

"Quiet!" Captain shouted back, half in anger, half in shock.

Strongheart stared wide-eyed and muttered, "You mean that's what happens when we…I mean, after a Ceremony of the Star, when we…."

"Yeah! Yeah, now you see!" said Muscles, nodding his sphere vociferously. "It's about time."

Captain turned around and peered back through the mist. Then he spun around abruptly and headed for the falls, almost at a trot.

19

Mission for Salvation

Safely back in their own valley, the seven members of the revenge mission huddled together with the other fifteen Mumwalds in Sage's cave. The warmth of their congregated bodies felt good.

No one spoke following Captain's report, not even Sage. In one respect the first stage of his plan had gone extremely well. In seven days the Torwinks should be getting quite weak from lack of food, according to his educated guess. He was excited about that, but his exhilaration was dulled by a twinge of guilt and sadness that continued to worm itself into his psyche despite himself. He wondered why he couldn't just accept the fact that revenge for the stoning of the peace mission and the killing of Motherfive was justified. He imagined Stargazer sitting next to him and prodding him with questions about the relationship of the revenge mission to sin.

But on his own, Sage did not feel up to exploring such weighty matters, and he wasn't even sure he wanted to discuss the subject with his protégé, for he had sensed, in the briefest of moments, that reasonable answers to the questions would not rule in favor of the Way of the Eagle.

The silence of most of the Mumwalds had nothing to do with deep thinking about sin and war. They were picturing to themselves what had been happening to Mumwald bodies all these years after they were sent over the falls. Motherone finally broke the silence with a quiet observation. "Isn't it ironic? All these years we've been providing the means for added comfort to the very ones who have now become our mortal enemies."

"Thank Great Maker we haven't yet sent Motherfive over the falls," said Mothersix with a shudder.

"Wha...oh...yes, of course," stammered Sage. He had been so engrossed with his plan that he was completely out of tune with the notes being struck in others' heads. "Yes, yes. We will certainly have to make some changes in how we handle our dead, won't we?"

Motherone nudged Stargazer and whispered, "He doesn't even feel the horror of it. He's all business."

Stargazer furrowed his brow.

Sage twisted his sphere from side to side, looking awkwardly about. "Well," he said, "are there other reactions to Captain's report?"

Strongheart spoke up. "Sage, what if the Torwinks had stored away a batch of the lily pads the way we've stored cones?"

"Ahhh," said Sage, relieved to be back to the plan. "A natural question. We used to have lily pads in our lake until a previous sage ordered them all cleared out because they were of no use and cluttered up the water. The pads, like other green plants, begin to dry out and wither once they are cut from their stems and taken out of water. There should be no way to keep them fresh for long."

"Do we have to wait for seven days before we go back?" asked Muscles.

"Yes," said Sage. "We want them thoroughly weakened

before we go back down to start gathering cones for storage
for winter." He looked squarely at Muscles. "And remember,
we're not going down there to kill Torwinks in direct fighting. I've planned this war so that none of us will risk getting
hurt."

"Aww," said Muscles. Motherfour tugged at his arm before he could go on. She whispered in his ear. He blushed
slightly, his lips curling in a smirk.

A tiny voice piped up. "Can I go on this next trip?"

Sage looked over beside Mothertwo. Mischief, still no
bigger than a lemon, was jumping up and down and waving
his arms.

"I could sneak into places where you big fatties couldn't
go," said the little creature.

Mothertwo was horrified. "Mind what you say, Mischief!"
she scolded. "Must I hold you upside down?"

"But it's true!"

"He may have a point," said Sage, "though his imperti-
nence gets too much exercise."

Mothertwo pursed her lips and said quietly, "Yes, Sage. I
try."

"Oh boy, you mean I can go then?" cried Mischief.

"I didn't say that, little one," said Sage. "We won't need
explorers on this next trip. But eventually we may need cones
from high in the trees, so perhaps we may need to send...."
He paused on his own.

Motherone's eyes narrowed. "You will not send Climber.
Not after—"

"Now, now, good mother! I didn't mean to get you stirred
up. It was just a thought that came to me on the spot. We will
determine later who will go."

"Yup, I'll bet I could play this game called war real good.
Yup, I could."

"I'm sure you could, Dumbell, but don't you think you
could help us more by staying up here and keeping our paths
clean?" The condescension in Sage's voice made everyone
look to the ground.

"Yup, if you say so, my good man. Yup." But a tear came
to Dumbell's eye. He didn't know if he would ever get the

chance to prove to Sage that he could do more than pick sticks off paths and sing silly songs.

Strongheart pulled them away from the awkward moment. "Sage, you haven't named the warm, foglike cloud rising out of the Torwinks' hot pools."

"Ah, yes. Let's see....We shall call it *steam.*"

For the next four days the Mumwalds tried to lead normal lives. They could never quite shake off a feeling of worry, though. The feeling lay there in their souls, stubbornly refusing to go away. The war wasn't the only thing bothering them. They were in the ninth day since Motherfive's death. The coming night would be the tenth since her Ceremony of the Star. The Wondrous Star hadn't been sighted, though the watch had been posted every night, even when it was cloudy and stormy.

In the late afternoon of that ninth day, rain came once again to the area. Sage saw that it was more than a quick shower. He sent a small party of Mumwalds into the valley of the Torwinks to see if the lily pads were still out of reach of the stick figures. They made a fast trip and reported that everything looked good. Sage smiled at the report and spoke confidently. "Three more days and we'll begin the next stage of the Way of the Eagle."

20

The Ceremony of War

As darkness came to the valley, the sky cleared. The watchers taking turns lying in the hollow of the stone were especially alert for the Wondrous Star. They didn't want the star to skim across the far edge of the sky unseen. But it was no use. Dawn came, and Stargazer, the last Mumwald on duty, had to report sadly that he hadn't seen the star.

Round bodies pressed together around the mouth of Sage's cave as the sky lightened. With somber faces they all heard Stargazer's bad news. The news troubled Sage more than he let on. The day before, he had been feeling good about the chances of the Mumwalds in the war. Now he wondered. Perhaps the failure of the star to come was a sign that things wouldn't work out well.

Still, he had the duty to lead the Mumwalds, to prepare their minds and bodies for war. He couldn't do that if they saw he was full of doubt.

Muscles growled, "Those Torwinks are a curse in every way. Wait until I get my hands on them!"

"Muscles, didn't you listen to what I said yesterday! No more killing!" Sage glared at the hate-filled male. Soon, though, his face softened. "Besides, we don't know that the Torwinks have any power over the Wondrous Star. We are truly saddened that the North Wind will take Motherfive to No Place. But this has happened before to the souls of other Mumwalds. It is one of those mysteries that the wisdom of the ages has no answer for. You would think that a fine mother like Motherfive...would...." His voice cracked. His eyes began filling with tears. Quickly, he scolded himself for letting himself wander down the path of sentimentality at a time like this. He took a deep breath and spoke anew with a quiet firmness. "Let us be sad without letting our minds be diverted either into undue grief or into rash anger."

Motherone, who had eased her way to the side of Stargazer, whispered to him. "I've never understood why we don't have a ceremony after someone is *not* picked up by the Wondrous Star. It seems—" Stargazer gently placed a finger in front of her mouth, for he saw that Sage was about to continue.

Before Sage could speak, however, Mischief's voice piped up yet again. "The star might've come if you'd said I could go to the war!"

Croaking twitters rippled through the crowd. Sage smiled at the little one despite his rudeness, for his remark had turned their thoughts exactly to the place Sage wanted them.

"Perhaps so, my brash young fellow," Sage said. "But I will not change my mind. The day after tomorrow will be the seventh day since our revenge mission. You all must use these last two days to prepare for our dawn venture. When the shadow of the west wall touches the east wall tomorrow evening, we'll have a final meeting in the theater."

All the Mumwalds except Captain and Strongheart scattered, their minds turned from Motherfive to the war. Sage didn't seem to notice the two lingerers. The weary old leader had closed his eyes and sat leaning his back against the cave wall.

"Sage," said Captain gently.

Sage's eyelids fluttered open. "Huh...mmm...oh, it's you two."

"Sorry, Sage, but before you rest we need some direction."

"Oh?"

Captain glanced at Strongheart, puzzled. Normally, Sage would have given the instructions the two were wondering about before they had a chance to wonder.

"What do we do with Motherfive's body? We can't take it out of the sanctuary and send it over the falls now, can we?"

"Oh, yes, I see what you mean. I suppose we shouldn't...or can't...or won't." With that he stopped and shut his eyes again.

Strongheart lifted his eyebrows and motioned with his hands for Captain to press on with the conversation.

Captain spoke hesitantly. He had never before had to drag instructions out of Sage. "Sage, the odor. When the wind is right, we....well...there have been some mild complaints. And if we leave her where she is longer, we...."

Sage's eyes popped open. A fierce scowl distorted his face.

"Take care of it! And let me be!" The eyes clamped shut. The scowl remained.

Slinking out of the cave, Strongheart and Captain slowly shook their spheres in unbelief. "What should we do?" asked the former, once they were outside.

"I don't think we'd better do anything yet. He's obviously overwhelmed by all that's going on. Maybe when he wakes up, he'll decide."

* * *

But Sage said nothing about the matter to Captain later that day or the next. Captain was afraid to bring it up himself. He would rather have the foul odor of rotting flesh seeping into his nasal passages than again feel the wrath of Sage.

The Mumwalds met in the theater the evening before the seventh day since the mission for revenge. Sage went over every step of their plan. In the end he said, "Now, to send us off properly to the last stage of the war, I have a surprise for you. I have created a new ceremony, the Ceremony of War. This may seem like an odd time to have such a ceremony, for we have already conducted the first mission of the war.

However, it has taken me much time and careful thought to create a new ceremony. This is not something I have merely called up from the wisdom of the ages. It is completely novel. It is a ceremony of guided, silent meditation. We will let the colors of the sky of the dying day speak to us. I will suggest ideas to your minds."

The audience stirred. One puzzled expression met another. Excited whisperings hissed through the crowd. Mischief opened his mouth to say something, but Mothertwo was ready for him. She quickly clamped a hand over his face and kept him quiet.

Motherone had no one to restrain her, but, of course, she only turned and whispered to Stargazer. "Is he getting creative in his old age? Or did you help him with this?"

Stargazer lifted one eyebrow. "I know nothing about it," he said. "Give the old boy some credit."

Motherone frowned skeptically as she said simply, "Ha! Maybe a certain stench has stimulated his brain! I hope this ceremony doesn't have much to do with Great Maker. Lately, I don't feel much like paying respects to Him."

Stargazer shifted uneasily on his stone slab. His lips pursed and his eyes squinted, but he didn't say anything.

"Well," said Motherone a bit defensively, "He's let things get way out of hand, wouldn't you say?"

A slight nod of his sphere was all the response Stargazer could muster. Motherone waited a few moments before she whispered again. "I think it is time I let you in on a little secret we females have. But we'll have to wait until after the ceremony."

Stargazer swiveled on his sphere to face her, but she looked straight at Sage with a faint, smug smile on her face.

Sage patiently had remained quiet for a couple of minutes to let everyone express feelings. Finally, he swooped his arms in an upward motion and said loudly, "All of you lie down on your backs and watch the sky, as we do in the Ceremony of the Star."

They all lay down, including Sage. He didn't know exactly what he was going to say or in what direction he would lead their thoughts. He was truly going to let the sky dictate ideas to him. Large tufts of clouds were wafting above them in the wind. The massive, soaring tops billowed high in gleaming whiteness.

"Think how fragile we are," said Sage in a quiet voice. "We are like the little puffs of yellow forming on the gray bottom of the clouds. We are but a fleeting, delicate strand floating on the underbelly of a huge mass of unknown."

As he smiled proudly to himself, Stargazer reached for Motherone's hand and squeezed it. He had never known his mentor to be so poetic, so contemplative. Were these new, troubling experiences enriching his mind, too?

The Mumwalds thought in silence. They watched the clouds merge into each other to form a more solid blanket above the valley. The sun still shone through a narrow slit out of the viewers' line of sight. In the west the blanket slowly became bright pink, melting into blues, purples and grays to the east.

"Think how fortunate we have been. For generations and generations our valley has been covered with peace, save for the occasional dark visit of an eagle or the misfortune of an accident."

The blanket lay still. Gradually, the light, bright pink darkened. Before long the western sky blazed in a somber blood-red.

Disturbing thoughts came to Sage. He hesitated to say anything. Finally, he felt he had to speak. "Tomorrow we hope to meet only Torwinks too weak for fighting. We pray to you, Great Maker, that the part of the war in which we inflict suffering on the enemy and they on us is over. We have planned according to the best knowledge we have. Yet, we may not fully succeed." His throat caught. He choked, then coughed. The corners of his eyes once again filled with water. His whole body shook. Still, he was determined to go on. With a mighty effort he held his voice firm.

"Though there is the slightest of chances that Mumwald blood may again be shed, we know it is for a good cause and with right reason. Therefore, my fellows, go forth with clear minds and stout hearts to do what you have to do."

The Mumwalds gazed silently at the changing cloud cover.

When only dark gray was left, Sage rose slowly. The others followed his lead and began to walk toward the caves, each alone in his thoughts. As they shuffled off hand in hand, Motherone turned to look at Stargazer. She wanted to ask him how he felt about the ceremony now, but his slightly narrowed eyes and tightly set lips told her to keep quiet.

Sage sighed deeply as he plodded along a few steps behind Captain. This was not the kind of send-off he had wanted. He was sure that his ceremony hadn't created the right feeling about being at war, whatever that feeling was supposed to be. *Ah, well,* he thought. *At least the ceremony had been honest and truthful, whatever good that might do for war.*

* * *

Motherone and Stargazer walked slowly enough that everyone else soon passed them.

"Well?" said Stargazer.

"Well, what?"

"Come on, quit being coy. What's your so-called female secret?"

"Oh, I thought you weren't in the mood to talk."

"Tell me something that will get my mind off war."

"I think what I have to say will do that. I...." The mother stopped walking. Stargazer felt a sudden tenseness in her hand. "But wait. It is strictly forbidden. I was hasty when I promised earlier," she muttered.

"Aww, come on now! What's forbidden? And by whom?"

"To tell you what I said I was going to. And by Healer."

"What does she have to do with this?"

"You males really don't know? You really don't? I was never sure Healer meant it when she said...."

"Will you please quit playing games?" Stargazer kept hold of her hand but stepped around in front of her. In the pale light he saw the deep concern in her eyes. "OK, OK. Take your time."

Motherone reached down to take hold of his other hand. She rubbed her thumb against his fingers for a few moments before she spoke. "We...we females have our own tradition."

"Huh?"

"We do. We have a tradition of our own, separate from the one handed down through sages. It comes to us through healers."

"You...you're not kidding, are you?" It was not really a question. Stargazer sensed her utter seriousness. "Is it much different from the wisdom of the ages that sages have?"

"In some ways, yes. And one way in particular is very relevant to our situation. You want to hear?"

"Of course."

"I guess Healer wouldn't mind as long as I have the ear of a male who is sympathetic to new ideas...so...." She took a deep breath and then blurted it out. "We don't think of our supreme being the same way you males do." That was all she could say for the moment. She looked intently into her lover's eyes. She saw only warmth and wonder. "You males like to think of Great Maker in terms of power—power to make all things, power to order whatever He wants, power to control everything if He wants to. We don't see Him that way. We don't even think raw power of that kind...how should I say it? It...it...pure power just isn't a laudable trait for our supreme being. There!" She stopped to catch her breath and to see what Stargazer might be ready to say. He said nothing. She went on, more slowly now. "Power, for us, must be in harmony with love and compassion. That's how we think of Great M...Maker. With great and tender care He tries to lead us along the right path in life. It's more like the way we nurture our young through encouragement and gentle nudges. He doesn't try to bludgeon us into His way. He uses per—"

"Hold on! Bludgeons? Who ever said Great Maker—even in the eyes of us males—bludgeons anyone?"

Motherone smiled peevishly. "Did I overstate how you view Him? Well, I apologize. As I started to say, we believe He moves us by persuasion, not by controlling power. He cajoles us toward the right way, lures us toward the good, comforts us in our times of pain."

"Holy trout flies! Do you realize what you are telling me? Do you remember the conversation we had in your cave the other night? You know, I was questioning Great Maker's power, and then Climber...."

"Yes, I had an urge to say something then but didn't have the courage to break our vow—oh, it isn't really a vow—the...the mutual agreement we females have had to keep our secret."

"So what are all you females doing when we have some ceremony involving Great Maker? Do you let your minds wander, or...you aren't laughing at us under your breath, are you?"

"My, my, no. We take all the ceremonies very seriously. In our minds we simply substitute our own name for Great Maker."

"And what is that? Something like 'Great Mother'?"

"Oh, Stargazer! That's exactly what we call Her!"

21

Ambush

An hour before first light in the morning, all the Mumwalds were gathered at the passage entrance. They were full of a good meal of cones, needles, and twigs. Sage had decided to send almost all the adults this time, and even three of the older young, for the danger was minimal and the more cone gatherers, the more cones gathered. After experiencing the ominous red sky the evening before, however, Sage had made one change in his plans. Not only was each Mumwald carrying a basket to collect cones in but also a shield. This would be cumbersome but was a prudent precaution.

Besides Sage, only Dumbell and Mothertwo would remain behind with the four young that weren't going. As the last adventurer disappeared into the passage, Mothertwo held tightly to Mischief so he wouldn't try to sneak along.

152

"Our food problem will soon be solved," said Sage, almost to himself. Even as he spoke, a quiver went through him. In his mind flashed a picture of Motherfive's soul sinking into No Place. Then an image of her decomposing body floating in the sanctuary popped into his mind, but he just as quickly dismissed it.

"I just wish I could help," said Dumbell with a long face.

"You can," said Mothertwo. "Why do you think we were kept behind?"

"Yup. I'm supposed to clean paths. Yup."

"No. Here, help me keep track of these young. I'll take my two and you take care of Climber and Motherfour's daughter."

Dumbell's eyes widened. Then, smiling broadly, he stretched out a finger from each hand for the two youngsters to grab hold of. "Righto," he said. Here was an unexpected task he had never before been allowed to do.

The other fifteen Mumwalds made their way down the passage, out through the falls, and into the pool. Rammer and Roller and Punky were having the time of their lives. In the pre-dawn darkness it was hard to see even the white-coated males. They hadn't bothered to coat themselves with mud this time. The flotilla bobbed downstream until they bumped into the bridge. One by one they climbed out of the water on the west bank, then crossed the bridge.

Suddenly, above the roar and splash of the falls, they heard the piercing whistle of a Torwink. Captain didn't say anything because he didn't want to make any more noise than necessary. So one Torwink had some strength left? Small worry.

Huddled closely together on the path in the darkness, the group wobbled as quickly down the path as they could. They came to the bend close to the Torwinks' lake. Captain silently stopped before they turned the corner, and the following Mumwalds shoved together in an even tighter mass.

After waiting a few more moments, Captain spoke. "All right. This is where we begin. We'll work back toward the falls from here, filling our baskets as full as possible. Then we'll swim back through the falls, dump our loads on the

ledge, and come back for more. We'll keep doing that until—"

"OK, OK," said Muscles. "Sage has already gone over the
plan. Can't we get started?"

The eastern sky was just beginning to lighten. The spooky
morning calm made several Mumwalds shiver. "I understand
your impatience, Muscles," said Captain. "But it's still rather
dark to see the cones. I was just stalling, to tell you the truth.
Either we started out too early or it didn't take as long for us
to get here as Sage thought. It shouldn't be—"

Two whistles, a short distance from each other, pierced
the air from close by, up in the trees.

"Humph," mumbled Captain. He couldn't ignore these,
but he wasn't sure what to say about them. "I wonder how
many of the Torwinks survived well enough without food to
be out and about?"

The Mumwalds shuffled restlessly, jostling each other and
murmuring doubts. Their squinting eyes searched the shadowy trees to no avail. Strongheart spoke above the din.
"Remember, it was a rock from the trees that mortally injured
Motherfive. We'd better be careful."

Another spoke up anxiously. "Shouldn't we find a spot to
wait away from the trees?"

"How about over by the boulder field that you described,
Captain?" said Motherfour.

"They have a large supply of rocks over there," Captain
said.

Muscles twisted his sphere with elbows extended to make
room for himself. He raised his shield. "What is it with you
sissies? We've come prepared for those devils. Let's get on
with our work! If they attack, we'll protect ourselves with the
shields and go after them!"

"If they are throwing from the trees, are you going to
climb up after them?" asked Stargazer, trying to keep his
contempt from showing in his voice.

Muscles merely sneered and then said, "We'll think of
something. Come on! We can begin to see cones now."

Captain hesitated another few moments, but no one else
offered any suggestions. "All right. Who knows? Some other

creature we don't know about may have made those whistles. Let's spread out on both sides of the path. But never get too far into the forest away from the path."

Earlier, the Mumwalds had imagined they would set their shields on the ground as they gathered cones into their baskets. Without being instructed to do so, every one of the balls of fur now held a shield tightly at the ready with one hand, set his or her basket on the ground, and used the other hand to pluck off cones.

By chance, Mothersix and her son Punky were the last pickers on the east side of the path. Not too many cones were on the lowest branches, the only ones the Mumwalds could reach. In the still dim light, they had to pause under each branch, feeling with their fingertips as well as looking with their eyes.

On the other side of the path from Mothersix and Punky was Muscles, with Motherfour only a few paces in front of him. As soon as Muscles stepped off the path, his gaze didn't go up to a branch but peered around at the forest floor. He quickly spotted what he was looking for. A few steps farther from the path brought him to a piece of broken-off branch about a foot long.

Setting down his basket and shield, he picked up the stick and patted it against his free hand. It wasn't quite as thick and heavy as the club he had back up in his own valley, but it would do for now. Smiling to himself, he retrieved his shield, slid the stick under that arm, lifted up his basket, and went to the task of finding cones.

The irregular columns of cone gatherers slowly worked their way up the long north-south stretch, not finding enough cones to fill their baskets quickly. Looking up through the branches, Mothersix saw a bright, clear sky emerging from the early morning gloom. More and more light penetrated to the forest floor, making the cones much easier to locate. Punky was not enthralled with the task at hand. With the increasing light, he found it possible to inspect a patch of lichen here, a grotesquely twisted tree branch there, a soft bed of needles a little farther on.

"Punky," called Mothersix. "Keep up with us. Quit lagging behind. And look there! You only have one cone in your little basket. You'll have to work harder than you are to get it full."

Punky mashed his lips outward and squinted in a pout, but he wasn't really upset. He wobbled up to his mother and kept right behind her for several minutes. Then an unusual rock jutting out of the forest floor caught his attention. It appeared that something had recently chipped away at the rock, exposing its insides on one side. Pretty veins of purple, gray, and white swirled in an exquisite pattern. Punky leaned forward to study the swirls, tracing along the curving lines with his finger, oblivious to odd scratching and rustling sounds coming from high in the trees.

Mothersix had gotten about ten feet ahead of him when she sensed that he was no longer with her. She turned to call him forward again. To her horror, she saw more than just Punky. Behind him, holding sticks raised above their heads ready to smash down on Punky, stood two Torwinks.

"Rrrooark!" Her guttural croak startled Punky and momentarily froze the Torwinks. The young Mumwald straightened up to see his mother pointing frantically at him. He turned his sphere just in time to see the Torwinks' sticks come unfrozen and start their downward arc toward his top. Instinctively, he let one leg go limp and began to roll over on one side. The two sticks smashed simultaneously into his left side, directly on the hearing mechanism.

Mothersix charged, her shield held out in front of her. "Get away from him!" she screamed. The Torwinks had no time for more blows. They scrambled toward the path.

At Mothersix's first cry, Muscles had grasped his club. His webbed feet flapped across the path toward the commotion just as the Torwinks burst out of the trees.

"They clubbed my Punky!" screamed Mothersix.

Muscles swung his club horizontally at the attackers. They adroitly leaned far backwards. The club swished right in front of their heads. Dropping their own sticks, they completed the backwards maneuver by doing a back flip. Before Muscles could swing back in the other direction, the Torwinks were dashing to the south on the arms-legs that had been holding the clubs only moments before.

With a rage-filled roar, Muscles waddled down the path after them. Captain and the other cone gatherers hurried out of the forest. "Muscles, come back!" shouted the leader. "What's going on? Come back here!" Muscles only seemed to increase his pace, if that were possible.

Strongheart looked at Captain. "Shall some of us go after him?"

Captain gazed down the path for a moment and shook his head. He swung his shield toward the trees where Mothersix hovered over Punky. All but Motherfour moved that way. She stared at her lover lumbering down the path amid great puffs of dust. "Muscles," she called weakly. "Muscles, please come back." He disappeared around the bend. Her eyes closed and her legs went limp, plopping her down on the soft dirt.

The others huddled around Punky and Mothersix. The young Mumwald lay motionless on his back, his eyes shut. Captain asked, "What happened? How badly is he hurt?"

Mothersix twisted to look up. The fur under her eyes was wet with tears. "Two Torwinks clubbed him," she said softly, "but he's alive, thank goodness. Blood is oozing out at his left ear covering."

Without warning, a small, jagged rock clipped Stargazer's arm. "Shields up!" he shouted. All the standing Mumwalds raised their shields flat above their heads, forming a roof over the injured young one. A few more stones pelted down, harmlessly bouncing off the tightly woven sticks.

Captain placed a soothing hand on Mothersix's. "Can he be moved?"

The good mother was softly stroking her son's top. The young one's eyes fluttered, then opened. He brought his left palm up and gently covered his hearing mechanism. "Ohhh," he groaned. Without saying anything, Mothersix took hold of his right arm and gave a slight upward tug. Punky responded by rolling onto his knees. With his mother steadying him, he remained kneeling for several seconds. Finally he boosted himself onto his feet and took a tentative step. "I think I can walk OK," he whispered. Without waiting for an order, the group started to shuffle toward the path, still holding their shields high.

Suddenly, an "Ouch! Oh! Oww!" came from Motherfour. The Torwinks in the trees had just discovered her and sent a flurry of little rocks down at her. She lifted her shield over her top and stood up just as Captain led the huddled mass of Mumwalds out from the trees. Most still carried their partially filled baskets. Captain did not order the others to go back into the forest to get theirs. An occasional stone plunked against the shield roof.

Captain took only a few seconds to make a decision. "We'll return to our valley," he said, "by the shortest route." Immediately, he marched in quick tempo off to the north on the path. Motherone and Mothersix flanked Punky, each grasping an arm to help him keep pace.

Motherfour stood still as the others marched away from her. "B-but, but, but," she stammered.

Stargazer reached a hand back toward her, and then stopped walking. "Don't get separated from us," he urged.

Motherfour was sobbing heavily. "C-c-couldn't we g-go the other way and…and maybe f-find my Muscles?"

Stargazer stepped back to her. He wished he had a free hand to grasp her with. "I'm afraid not." He spoke with quiet firmness. "It would be too risky. Muscles is strong. He'll probably meet us at the falls." He swung his basket around behind her and nudged her along. Slowly they picked up their pace. The large group had slowed down; before long the entire troop was reunited and heading determinedly toward the stream, looking from the top a bit like a Roman phalanx but feeling more like frightened, straggling refugees from a war zone. Without further hassles, other than the annoying peppering of rocks against their shields, they reached the stream and then the falls. Muscles did not meet up with them. Reluctantly, Captain ordered them to proceed up the passageway and out into their own valley.

22

The End of Sage

Sunlight still had not reached the valley floor when the first of the returning party stumbled out of the passageway into the meadow. Over where the main path neared the lake, Mothertwo and Dumbell sat idly, facing away from the passage entrance, their backs against a rock. The four youngsters in their charge were drawing with sticks in the dust on the path. Sage was not with them, for he had retired to his cave for more rest as soon as the cone gatherers had disappeared.

Mischief was the first to see Mumwalds straggling out of the passageway. "Yippee! They're back!" he shouted, not being close enough to see their dejected demeanors. The little fellow immediately took off running toward the caves. "I'll go get Sage!"

Mothertwo and Dumbell made no attempt to stop him. They stood and turned around. Instead of seeing a line of Mumwalds marching proudly and excitedly toward them with baskets brimming with cones, they observed a deathly quiet, loose crowd facing the entryway, apparently waiting until the last member of the party had emerged. Mothertwo looked at her companion and squeezed down her eyebrows.

"Yup, doesn't look good, my lady. Yup," said Dumbell softly.

As the two stood silently, the crowd turned and lumbered toward them in scattered formation. Mothertwo tried to count to see if all fifteen were there, but the shifting, disorderly mass made an accurate count impossible. At least she could see three small spheres bobbing along. She wondered why Punky

held on to his mother with one hand and covered his left hearing mechanism with the other, but she was relieved to know that he and Rammer and Roller were safe. As the group trudged closer, she became aware that some held baskets and some didn't, and the baskets that were in view were not overflowing with cones. Suddenly she caught a glimpse of Motherfour shuffling along in the rear. On one side of her was Stargazer and on the other was Motherone. Mothertwo frantically scanned the whole group for Muscles. His solid bulk was missing. Mothertwo padded over to Motherfour's little daughter, who was staring at the approaching Mumwalds, and gently drew her close.

Captain was the first to come up to the small group of spectators. He darted a glance at the adults, blinked, and then

plopped himself down on his bottom in the middle of the path. He leaned his sphere forward and gazed blankly into the dirt. As the others plodded up, they followed suit, all except the last trio. Stargazer and Motherone each held an upper arm of Motherfour, whose front fur below the eyes was soaked with tears. With a heaving sigh, she shook loose her supporters, knelt in the dust, and held out her hands toward her daughter. Timidly, with teardrops welling up in her own eyes, the little female inched into her mother's grasp. After a prolonged squeeze, the small one pushed away just far enough to allow her rolled-up eyes to look at her mother's closed, glistening eyelids. "Where's Daddy?" she whispered. "I—I don't see Daddy."

Motherfour couldn't speak. She gave a slight side to side twist to her sphere and again tightened her hug.

Finally, Captain asked Mothertwo to inform Sage of their return. She was about to answer when they all heard a loud, jovial, "Ho, there! Back so soon?" Sage, propelling himself faster than usual with a walking stick, and Mischief rushed into view on the path from the caves.

Moments later Sage's exuberant mood was sobered by Captain's report, stammered out in short, hushed bursts. After Captain finished, a long silence enveloped the valley. No breeze stirred the trees. No note of a bluebird song sounded. No chipmunk squeak piped up. At last, with no other words, Sage asked Stargazer to help him back to his cave. The other Mumwalds were left to brood in bewilderment.

Sage did not speak to his pupil all the way back to his shelter. As they came out of the trees, they saw that bright sunshine was now warming the cliff wall clear to the valley floor. The old leader trudged up to the cave entrance and sat down with his back against the comforting rock. He motioned for Stargazer to sit beside him. "I do not understand what is going on," he said softly. "But I do know one thing. I cannot bear more of this."

"Time will help," said Stargazer.

"No. No, not this time. Motherfive's death nearly did me in. Now Muscles' disappearance and Motherfour's anguish is more than I can take."

"But you haven't—"

Sage weakly raised a hand to stop Stargazer. "Please, just listen. You must prepare yourself to take over the leadership of the Mumwalds. I shall die within little more than a week. Yet I have much more received wisdom to pass on to you. You and I must spend most of our time together in the next few days. For this concentrated effort, I will need all my energy. I do not want to be disturbed by having to make any more decisions for the good of our clan. You are to be acting sage from now on, and you will have the name as soon as I'm gone. You will need to communicate your wishes to Captain when and as you see fit. Right now I want to go inside and rest and get my thoughts and memories in order. You go conduct any business you think necessary and come back here when the sunlight half fills the valley." At that, he took Stargazer's hand in his and clasped it tightly. The two continued to stare out at the forest. "You will make a wonderful sage, my son, but circumstances will be most trying for a time. Go now. Do what you have to do. And may Great Maker watch over you." With that, Sage pushed himself up laboriously and wobbled into the cave.

Stargazer found himself speechless. He sat for many minutes while a rush of thoughts and emotions charged through him. Slowly, the first actions that he must take crystallized in his mind. He got up and walked pensively toward the lake, where most of the Mumwalds had remained, to tell Captain to post watches at the passage entrance day and night and to dispose of Motherfive's body in a novel way, by burying it where the forest met the meadow directly west of the theater. They would give the Torwinks no more Mumwald hides. No one seemed surprised that Stargazer was now giving the orders.

When he had finished, he stepped over to Motherone, took her hand, and led her off the path for a walk through the forest. Behind them, by the lakeside, Jester and Dumbell were calling all the Mumwald young together for water games. They had decided on their own that the young needed this diversion and the mothers needed time away from their young to deal with the situation. The chattering of the players pierced the somber cloud that had settled on the valley. Stargazer abruptly began to hum the tune to Dumbell's "Boom, boom, ain't it great to be crazy" song.

Motherone brushed aside the tip of a spruce branch. Her eyes shifted to look sideways at her companion. "You're in an odd mood for the times," she said.

"Hmm? Oh...I...." He turned and looked at her sheepishly. "I guess I'm rather enjoying being in charge."

"But there is so much pain within us all right now."

"Yes, yes, I know." And he quit humming.

As if Motherone's words had conjured the image, they suddenly became aware that another Mumwald, a gray-furred one, was ahead of them, plodding through the forest in the same direction. The way the female sphere was tilted forward and each webbed foot was laboriously being dragged forward told them who it was.

"Motherfour," called Motherone softly.

Motherfour stopped but did not turn around. The other two Mumwalds dropped hands and came up to her from behind. Each placed the palm of a hand against her back and began gently rubbing. No one spoke. The quiet sobs of the grieving Mumwald formed a strange counterpoint to the still audible chatter of the young playing on the lake. After some moments Stargazer pointed toward two small spruce logs that had fallen long ago to form a V. They had rotted enough that the prickly bark had fallen off.

The Mumwalds moved over to them and sat down, the two mothers side by side on one and Stargazer facing them on the other.

Motherone broke the silence. "Maybe Muscles will come back yet. He is so strong."

Motherfour heaved a sigh and gave a feeble nod of her sphere. She looked at Stargazer and mumbled, "What's happening to us? I...I...can't make any sense out of it."

The new leader squinted for a moment. "I've been doing a lot of thinking about what's been going on these past couple of weeks. A lot of terrible things have been happening to us. And we don't seem to have deserved them." He bit his lip. Muscles' recent attitude and actions didn't fit with that last statement, but this wasn't the time to get into that. "But...but maybe not all that has been going on is as bad as it seems at first."

Motherfour's sobs stopped and she looked him straight in the eyes with a fierceness that made him shudder. Stargazer gave a quick, questioning glance to Motherone. She responded only with a widening of her eyes and a slight tilt of her sphere. He took that as a signal to go on.

He looked at the mothers' webbed feet as he talked. He couldn't think well when he looked directly at them. "Don't get me wrong, Motherfour. Some things that have happened are undeniably bad and very difficult to understand—the cone blight, the whole conflict with the Torwinks resulting in Motherfive's death...and now Muscles' disappearance. To be honest, I don't know for sure yet how to come to terms with some of these events. But the cone blight seems to be a bit different from the other two. After all, the orange growth was only trying to fulfill its own destiny. It just happens that its destiny and ours have come into conflict. The more I think about it, the more it seems true—our world is simply made in such a way that when one set of events tries to do its thing, it may come into conflict with another set of events trying to do its thing. And suffering may be the result." He paused and looked up at Motherfour. The fierceness was gone from her countenance. She seemed to be hearing what he was saying.

"You see," he continued, "a few days ago Motherone and I had a conversation in which a rather startling idea came out. We discovered that something positive was coming out of some of our suffering. Take Sage and me—we had been getting into some discussions that got rather heated, at least for us. We both were feeling uncomfortable, even a little bit betrayed and rejected by the other. But the odd thing is, later I realized that these confrontations had made me start doing some very creative thinking. I...I feel I have begun to come up with some more meaningful explanations for what is happening. I actually now believe that these difficult discussions have enriched my life by letting some novelty into it. I suppose if we could retain completely the same old routines without disruption day after day, year after year, we might never suffer; but neither would we know the thrill of discovering new thoughts and new feelings."

He stopped again. Motherfour's mouth was opening. "Oh, my, my," she murmured. "So some suffering is good in the long run." She paused. "But my Muscles...." She couldn't go on.

Motherone clasped her seatmate's hand tightly. "You're right," she said quietly. "The situation with Muscles doesn't fit into this business of positive suffering very well. We just don't know yet what's become of him, and that makes it very hard." She squeezed Motherfour's hand again. "Stargazer is talking more about something like what happened to Ancientone. Her passing was tragic in a way. But she had lived a full life, and her passing freed resources that can better be used to nurture and sustain new Mumwald life. If...if Climber had died in the clutches of the eagle, that would have caused negative suffering. Something very valuable would have been lost before its full contribution to the process of life had been made." This time after she stopped, she didn't feel like saying any more, and neither did the other two.

Finally, Motherfour stood up off the log. "I thank you both. You've helped me. I can see I need to have patience. Maybe Muscles will...will...I think I'd like to continue my walk now alone." She slowly stepped away into the forest.

When she was out of earshot, Stargazer said, "Did we really help her?"

"Oh, yes, I think so. She won't only be focusing on Muscles now. And she will get much comfort from Great Mother. We always do." That slight, smug smile slipped onto her face.

With that, the two continued to sit for a long time in silence. Eventually, Stargazer mused, "We live in a world in which suffering is inevitable. Many experiences probably have a combination of positive and negative suffering—such as the cone blight situation and even our confrontations with the Torwinks. Both jarred us out of the triviality of our previous experiences, and that's good. But both have also resulted in too much discord, too much...well, obviously much negative suffering has engulfed us. And that is truly evil. So many of our experiences are a mixture of good and evil. What we need in life are constructive contrasts—differences that generate gentle tensions in us, that...that don't split apart the fundamental harmonies that hold our individual beings together. What we don't need are jarring conflicts that destroy too much of our inheritance from the past, that split us apart from what we have been. I guess we can take only so much novelty."

"But we need some!"

"Oh, yes! It's just that...." He shook his sphere from side to side. "The...the right balance between triviality and discord may not always be easy to find."

With that, they sat in silence for some time. Finally, Stargazer said, "You know, our old way of thinking that we could eliminate suffering if we eliminate sin is unrealistic. Being sinless removes some negative suffering, but sinlessness neither does away with positive suffering nor with negative suffering that comes from non-sinful occurrences, such as the cone blight. Our ancestors didn't take into account the totality of our experience."

Motherone shoved off her log. She reached both hands out to Stargazer. "No, they didn't," she said. "And we are going to have to change that!"

* * *

The next eight days passed quickly. Stargazer spent most waking hours in Sage's cave, listening with wonder and admiration as his exhausted mentor poured out the remaining contents of his memory. On the ninth morning Stargazer entered the cave once more, but this time an ominous quiet was all that met him. Sage had died in his sleep. A Ceremony of the Star was held that night for the revered leader, and the Wondrous Star was sighted within an hour. Sage was buried next to Motherfive, and a chunk of stone was placed over each *grave*, as Stargazer, now Sage with a capital *S*, named them.

Muscles had not appeared. Since Stargazer had been so busy, Motherone and Healer had been ministering closely to Motherfour. They had reported regularly to Stargazer on the bereaved one's condition. The day after old Sage's death, new Sage decided that the watch at the passage entrance could finally be given up without causing a worsening of Motherfour's emotional state. Sage ordered the big stone slab rolled over the entryway. Yet another Ceremony of the Star was held for the presumed dead Muscles. No Wondrous Star was observed that night.

23

Suicide?

The next morning Sage woke up earlier than usual. Still, he was one of the last to get up. He shuffled to his new cave entrance for a good stretch and yawn in the brisk air. Dumbell was just disappearing down the path into the trees, headed for the lake to start some morning chore. Sage went back into the cave. He stepped to one of his cone bins in the rear and rummaged down through the cones, squeezing several with his hand until he came to one that felt right. His strong teeth ripped off a chunk. He closed his eyes as he munched on it, savoring the taste.

A faint shout came from outside. He turned to look out the entrance as he bit off another hunk. More shouts—and they seemed to be getting closer. He sauntered toward the bright light. Suddenly the words of the shouting became clear. "My good man! My good man!" Sage let the arm with the cone fall to his side. He peered down the lake path. Dumbell burst into view, stumbling and wildly waving his arms. "My good man! My good man!"

"What is it, Dumbell?" shouted Sage back with an amused smile. What little crisis has the slow one come up against now, he wondered?

Dumbell stopped running and gasped for breath. He gulped in a batch of air and yelled once more. "Come quick!" Then he turned around and rumbled back toward the lake.

Sage looked over to other Mumwalds who had been puttering about outside their caves. They returned the look quizzically. He lifted his arms palms up in as much of a shrug as a Mumwald could give. Sage started off at a slow waddle toward the lake. Dumbell popped out of the trees again without any warning. "Hurry!" he yelled, then whirled and sped off in the opposite direction.

Sage increased his waddle several notches. When he came out of the trees at the lake he found Dumbell at the edge of the water looking back toward him, urging him on with his right arm but pointing his left out into the lake. Even in the sunless light Sage could see a white blob floating dangerously close to the falls.

"Who is it?" he asked as he came up to Dumbell.

"Yup! I don't know, my good man. Yup!"

"Has he moved since you first saw him?"

"Yup! Nope! Yup!"

"I take that for a no."

"Yup, my good man."

Motherone and several other Mumwalds arrived. Sage pulled Motherone aside. "This doesn't look good. I must swim out there and find out what's going on." He looked straight at her. "Will you come with me? And do you think we should bring Healer along too?"

"I'll come." Then Motherone twisted her sphere from side to side. "But Healer? She's very good at many of the arts of healing, but I think I know what this may be all about, and...and she's too much like old Sage—kind of stuck in an old mind-set—to do much good here."

Sage was puzzled, but this was no time for hesitation. He

grabbed her arm and tugged her into the water. "The rest of you stay close by the shore in case we need help," he hollered to the crowd.

As soon as the two were away from the shore, he said, "What did you mean, you think you know what this is all about?"

"Nobody has wanted to bother you the last few days with all you've had to do. But several of us have been concerned about Sneaky. It didn't seem like a major crisis, so we...now I wish we'd said something."

"So that's Sneaky out there?"

"I'd bet on it."

They swam steadily toward the solitary figure. Motherone told Sage what little she knew. Ever since Motherfive's death, several Mumwalds had commented that Sneaky hadn't seemed like his old self. Some withdrawal was to be expected, of course, but the way he had snapped at others the few times he had had to communicate had given a hard edge to his depression. Motherone, Jester, and Healer had all tried to get him to sit and talk out his feelings. He had rather rudely rejected all such opportunities. He hadn't threatened harm to anyone or to himself, but he was like a Mumwald who'd been holding his breath a long time—something had to give.

They were getting closer. The floating blob was, indeed, Sneaky. He faced the falls, only the distance of a tall spruce tree from the precipice. To keep from being pulled over by the gentle current, his webbed feet and both hands backpaddled in slow, steady rhythm.

When the rescuers were a short cone's throw from him, they stopped paddling forward. "Sneaky," said Sage, no louder than he had to.

The moving limbs stopped, but only for an instant. "Leave me alone!"

"Motherone's with me. We want to talk."

"Go to No Place! And leave me alone!"

The two let themselves drift a bit closer. "We're not leaving," said Motherone soothingly. "We'll just swim around to your front so you can see us."

"No you don't! Stay where you are!" Sneaky took two powerful forward strokes, propelling him closer to the falls. He stopped with those and began backpaddling again.

"OK, OK," said Sage. "We'll stay back here. Please talk to us." He paused only briefly. "What's going on?"

"Are you an idiot? Can't you see I'm getting ready to take the big plunge! Heh, heh. By the Wondrous Star, maybe this'll catch Great Maker's attention. Nothing else has."

Sage arched his eyebrows at Motherone. "What does Great Maker have to do with this?"

"Aww, come on, Star...er, Sage. You and old Sage are the ones who've filled us full of all those hokey pokey ideas about Great Maker! All-powerful! Has the power to do anything He wants to do! Wants us to have the good life and...." He sniffled loudly with his nose. "And...and will take care of us if we do what we're supposed to! What a bunch of cold north wind!" He lifted one hand out of the water and swiped at his eyes.

"Go on, Sneaky," said Motherone softly.

"You know how it's been! Why should I have to tell you?"

"We want to hear exactly what you are thinking."

"We were doing everything right." He sniffled again. "We were being as good as we knew how. Old Sage said so! And this orange stuff comes out of nowhere, and the Torwinks beat us up and even kill my Moth...." His sphere was vibrating up and down in the water. "Then...then Muscles goes crazy with hate. Good grief, you two, can't you see? Great Maker's let us down! Or He's lost control! Or He's forgotten about us! Maybe one more death will wake Him up—or serve Him right." His voice got very quiet. "I...I...don't know....I just want it all to end." He stopped paddling altogether and started drifting toward the falls.

"Sneaky, wait! We agree with you...about Great Maker, I mean!" said Sage.

Sneaky braked. Slowly, he turned around to face them. They could see the redness in his eyes. "You what?"

"What you said about Great Maker. We agree with you—more or less. Hold on! We'll explain." He stopped for a moment. "Can I go ahead?"

Sneaky rubbed the back of a hand across his nose and tilted his sphere in a nod. He took two stronger strokes in their direction, then went back to paddling just enough to stay in the same place. They eased forward. They were only an eagle's wing spread apart now.

"We...Motherone and I...we've been doing a lot of thinking and talking since all this began happening. We believe the wisdom of the ages has passed along some ideas about our supreme being that make no sense. The tradition said Great Maker had the raw, absolute power to completely control the world whenever He wanted to. But then all this suffering came to us, and He did nothing. We don't think it helps a bit to say that we simply don't understand the reasons for what's happening. The way we thought of Great Maker...well, we are onto a better way to picture our supreme being. We can conceive of a being greater than one like Great Maker—a being with the tremendous power of love and compassion."

"So...you're saying that we've been worshiping the wrong supreme being all these years?"

"Not the wrong supreme being—we simply have had some wrong ideas attached to the one and only supreme being. The true one wills only good things for us. But...stay with me here...this is the tricky part...the true one does not have the power to control everything that goes on in the world. And the—"

Motherone broke in. "Let me take over." Sage made a sweeping gesture with one hand. "Sneaky," said the mother. "We mothers have had another set of ideas for the supreme being for ages, but we've never been allowed to use it except among ourselves. Great Mother is Her name."

"Great Moth...Moth...?"

"Yes! She doesn't rule us with controlling power. For goodness sake, we all know that we can do things on our own. Maybe they are just little things compared with what Great Mother can do. But we do make thousands of little choices in our lives that really make a difference in what happens in the future. Think about it. Mothertwo decides to hold Mischief upside down for being rude, and that helps his character fit the Mumwald mold. Sage decides that we search for cones in a new valley, and...and...so the point is, we do have some freedom that we can use to help shape the world."

"S-so what? What good does that do us?"

"It helps show that Great Mother doesn't control—can't control—every little thing that goes on in our lives."

"But what's the use of even making all these little decisions if bad things are going to happen to us no matter what we do?"

Motherone scrunched her face in thought for a moment. "You are asking tough questions, Sneaky. We can't always avoid tragedy and the suffering that goes with it. What we should try to do with our free choices is preserve the value in our old ways and create some new value in whatever ways we can—try to do good and to be good in new ways so that we enhance our lives and the life of Great Mother."

"Great Moth...Mother?"

She paddled up very close to Sneaky. He didn't move.

"That's right. She influences us and other events, but She doesn't have the power to control us or other events completely. Goodness, She couldn't have all the power in the world. If She did, we creatures wouldn't even have the power to exist! We'd simply be some kind of extension of Her."

Sneaky's somber stare turned to Sage. "Do you believe all that she's been saying?"

Sage hesitated only a second. The ideas Motherone had been spouting needed a bit of refinement here and there, he was sure, but not at this moment. "Yes!" he said firmly.

"So really," Sneaky said with wonder, "Great Mother comforts us and tries to persuade us to do the right thing, but...but each one of us and the orange fuzz and the horrible Torwinks...we're all these little power centers that she can't totally control." He was almost smiling. "Ha! That might work! This whole business wasn't Her fault. She was in there trying to make good things happen, but other things mucked up Her plan. Ha!"

Sage drifted up to Sneaky. He and Motherone got on either side of the troubled male but didn't touch him yet. "Shall we swim back to shore?" asked Sage.

"OK. But I am so tired." He let out a huge sigh. The two rescuers each placed an arm against his back, and all six webbed feet began stroking toward the waiting crowd.

24

Toward the Unknown

One bright, quiet day a week or so later, Sage and Motherone took a leisurely stroll to the lake. It was mid-morning. Sunlight glinted on the water as they came out of the forest. They walked to the lakeshore and found a flat rock large enough for both of them to sit on. Sage brushed off some dried remains of mudballs. They sat down. A deep-blue, cloudless sky formed a soothing dome over them. No other Mumwalds were close by.

After enjoying the peaceful scene for some time, Motherone said, "It's been nice to have a week without any great traumas."

"Yes, it has."

"How are you coming with Sneaky?"

"Oh, so-so. After the first euphoria of hearing about Great Mother, he's had a letdown. His allegiance to the old

175

idea of Great Maker is deeply held, yet...yet he can't get rid of those rebellious feelings either. I'm not sure how he'll come out in the end."

"Hmm. At least Motherfour is perking up slowly."

"Remember, though, the Wondrous Star hasn't picked up Muscles yet. If it doesn't come in the next couple of days, will that set Motherfour back?"

"Oh, I hardly think so. We mothers haven't taken that ten day business seriously for generations."

Sage chuckled. "I should have guessed." After a pause, he wondered aloud, "We Mumwalds have never been as harmonious as some of us have thought, have we?"

Motherone squirmed on her seat. "We females never had the spirit of true rebels." Her eyes looked far away. "Now, if we could only get Sneaky and Motherfour interested in each other."

"They don't seem to me to be much attracted to each other."

Motherone sighed. "Nor to me. Could you give them a good, hard nudge?"

"All the received wisdom says compulsion rarely works."

"Yes, I'm sure. Well, at least the pall that has been hanging over our valley seems to be lifting for most of us."

"I agree. If we can only manage to collect enough good cones for this winter, maybe we'll be set for a time....Maybe events will begin again to glide smoothly over the glossy surface of time."

Motherone smirked. "Now, now. You don't want that surface to be too glossy—remember, it's the little rough spots that add a bit of a zing to life!"

"Humph," he said. He looked out through the notch in the cliff where the falls plummeted. The horizon was jagged with distant, hazy mountains. He had never given much thought to those mountains. But now...an uncertain future...unknown places...and who would guide them? If not Great Maker, then Great Mother, or...?